Cuffed is w

As an own

ensure that some of the ....

result in harm to our members, their guests, and staff. Or at least I provide Band-Aids and salve to the dominants when kissing the boo-boos isn't enough. We try not to let anything worse than that occur.

I'm a full-time healer, love the violet wand, and stay very busy to avoid thinking about the worst parts of my life. My late omega and the child he carried. The lie that cost me everything. No, I come here to forget the pain. And the fact that I will never again have someone in my life. Fate already ripped my heart to shreds with her first gift. There will not be a second.

Such a Sweet Omega is the fifth book in His Alpha Desires, the highly anticipated M/M Mpreg shifter series by USA Today Bestselling Author Lorelei M. Hart and featuring the members and staff of the hottest new club in town. Such a Sweet Omega features an alpha club owner who's already lost everything and doesn't want to hurt again, the one omega who

Lorelei M. Hart

can change that, sweet heat, sizzling heat, new beginnings, finding oneself, true love, fated mates, an adorable baby (or two) and a guaranteed HEA.

Lorelei M. Hart

Digital ISBN: 979-8-89320-163-5

Print ISBN: 979-8-89320-164-2

His Alpha Desires Series

Such a Good Omega

Such a Lovely Omega

Such a Brave Omega

Such a Delicious Omega

Such a Sweet Omega

Such a Feisty Omega

Such a Sweet Omega

By

Lorelei M. Hart

Chapter One

Jabez

I shouldn't have driven home.

After the near disaster that occurred that night, every one of my triggers, well, triggered. Most shifters used midwives for their births, or healers who specialized, and after my past, I chose not to take on such cases, specializing in other types of healing.

"Come quickly!" the caller announced. "There's an omega about to give birth right on the street, and there are humans gathering."

In most cases, human and shifter omegas gave birth in very similar ways with one large difference. A fair percentage of our children arrived in their animal form. It didn't last long, and few would shift again for at least several years, but for those first moments, their alpha and omega dads would get a peek at what their child would look like when they got old enough to take their fur...or feathers or scales.

It was a blessed moment and one shifter parents looked forward to with great pleasure, but since many humans did not know we existed, someone needed to, "Get that omega out of the street." I shouldn't even have to say it. "Are you near a birthing center?"

"I don't think so," the person on the other end said, "but they aren't exactly in the mood to be moved far."

"How about a motel? Hotel? Anywhere under cover?"

"There is a motel just down the street. Want me to see if they have enough money for it?"

"Oh good gods. Tell me where you are, and I'll meet you at the place and pay for a night. Keep the omega out of sight though. No innkeeper is going to be thrilled to have someone giving birth in their room."

The other party chuckled, cutting through their frantic tone. "I guess that's pretty messy, huh?"

"I suppose you could say that." I was already getting dressed as we spoke. "I will likely be charged a cleaning fee." I took down the address of the motel and, just in case, the place where the omega was currently, in case he was not moveable at all. Then I disconnected, promising to hurry.

Jaw tensed, I unlocked it enough to take two quick breaths and let the air whoosh out. My mind raced as I sought any possible alternative to attending the birth. But I couldn't think of anyone who was closer to the location than I was, and neither my oath nor my conscience would permit me to do anything less than my best in this situation. A life—two lives or maybe even more, since shifters often had multiples—lay in the balance. My own issues would have to be put aside while I did my job.

My. Job.

Preferences and neuroses could not come into the picture, or I'd have to hang up my stethoscope.

I pulled up in front of the motel to find a skinny wolf shifter just past adolescence leaning against a wall. Rather, he was skinny except for the tremendous bump jutting out from his middle. Even at this distance and with the building's shadow hiding his features, I could tell he'd been getting far too little to eat, making his stamina questionable. He looked barely of age, maybe one of the runaways who left their pack and ended up in all kinds of trouble.

3

Another male, this one equally young and equally lean, hovered in front of the motel's office door under the registration sign. I offered a friendly smile to the pregnant wolf and joined the other one.

"You came in time!" he breathed. "I didn't know what I'd do if you didn't. Rally is..."

"Your friend?" I guessed. "You take care of each other...on the streets?" It wasn't difficult to ascertain; they were both filthy, shoes worn, and jeans torn. I'd seen kids like this before. "He's all you have."

Tears sprang into the young man's eyes, his gaze dropping to the ground between us, but he said, "Yes. Can you save him?"

"I don't know anything about the situation yet, but let's get a room and get him settled in bed so I can examine him and we'll see what we can do."

The motel owner's derisive expression told me he saw me with this young man and had decided I was one of the older wolves who took advantage of Rally and his friend or those like them. It was difficult not to correct him, but since we were about to make a mess of one of his

4

rooms, I let him judge me. He probably saw situations like that often. It made me shudder to think, but I suppressed it and accepted the key.

Picking up the pregnant omega, Rally, on the way, we soon were in the room, safely behind closed doors. I gave him a quick exam and had him get into the shower for sanitation's sake. While he was scrubbing off the layers of street filth, I ordered food delivery for them both. They needed the nourishment. If I was guessing right, the food would still be hot when the delivery was in the past.

The other omega, who finally told me his name was Ouro, took Rally's place in the shower, and I checked again to see how soon the babe would be arriving.

"Looks like we don't have long to wait," I said, sitting beside him on the bed. "Are you hoping for a boy or girl?"

"I just hope I can find a way to feed them because I don't have...don't have..." Tears leaked from his eyes. "I will have to put them up for adoption."

"Would it make you feel better if I told you I know of a place for you and your baby to go after they are born?"

"But what about..."

"Ouro, too. It's a very lovely home in the suburbs that helps out young wolves who are far from home and need to get on their feet. And if you decide adoption is the best choice, they can help with that, too. But I have a feeling that's not what you want to do."

"I want to do the best for my baby, and the life I live is not that. But"—the faintest trace of hope colored his voice—"you really think I might be able to find a way to keep them and not ruin their life?"

"Yes. The couple who runs the place are good friends of mine. They've helped quite a few people over the years. So, all you have to do right now is breathe and push when I tell you. Okay?"

It should have been that simple.

Chapter Two

Beale

I was stuck between knowing I deserved better and being tired of dating. Breakups were hard. Starting over, dating someone new was even harder. Of course, my wolf wanted me to stay single and wait forever for my fated mate, but life didn't work that way sometimes.

So when Aaron texted me, wanting me to go to Cuffed again, I put the phone down and didn't immediately reply.

I didn't know what to say. There was something off about Aaron. I couldn't put my finger on the red flags about him, but my wolf and my gut told me to be careful.

My wolf had never steered me wrong, but I was also tired of being alone.

At my age, I thought I would already be happily mated with pups on the way. My desperation was making decisions for me and, lately, I didn't know if they were good ones.

Aaron's thick lips and dark, beady eyes were the first signs, but I chalked up my dislike of those characteristics to watching too many crime documentaries. Still, it felt like he was holding his real self back. I got glimpses of anger bubbling from underneath his smooth and overly kind demeanor. Felt it in the air like a charge of electricity but again, my growing anxiousness about being unmated tugged me back into his embrace.

All week, I'd debated with myself about breaking it off.

Cutting ties with him, even the idea of it, gave me some peace in my soul. That should've been a sign.

The other issue was, I liked Cuffed. It was a place where I felt safe for a moment or two. Where even if Aaron got overly dominant, he would never hurt me. Dungeon monitors oversaw the different areas, making sure no one got hurt, at least, in ways they didn't want to.

Aaron wanted to try everything in the beginning but had gravitated toward knife play.

It scared me at first, but the way the alphas and omegas interacted in the demos and scenes made me think it wasn't so bad.

Tonight, Aaron planned a scene for the two of us.

My fear should've made me decline—cancel the date.

Goddess only knew why after a few minutes of arguing with myself that I agreed, saying that I'd meet him at the club in a few hours. He never picked me up for our dates. There were no flowers or sweet morning texts.

Dating Aaron had been rather cold and contractual.

Too bad I preferred that over being alone.

I ate dinner early since Aaron only wanted to see me at the club or his house. He never asked me to spend the night, and a smidgeon of pride stopped me from asking to stay.

I'd had iced lattes that were warmer than him.

The more I mulled over it, the more I regretted not breaking up with him.

One more time, I told myself. This date would be the make or break with him.

Dressed in my leather harness and black tight pants, I threw on a peacoat for the walk to the club. I would have to be there early and wait for Aaron to arrive. He had the membership, so I couldn't enter without him.

"Hey," a man waiting outside said to me. "Waiting for someone?" He was vaping and had a mask pulled up, resting on top of his head. It was one of those masks that resembled a futuristic soldier. I'd seen some of those guys on social media. They were hot, but that simply wasn't my thing.

"I am." I bundled my jacket tighter around me.

"He's with me." Aaron's voice boomed from behind me. He got his ticket and thrust his keys at the omega valet with no finesse whatsoever. Valet parking at the club was a new thing, and I'd heard other omegas saying that the club had purchased the parking garage a block over.

Aaron once made a comment about omegas talking too much.

The more I thought about it, the more I wanted to go home and curl up with a good book. The pages would've been nicer than him.

"Ready to go in?" he asked, grabbing my elbow and tugging me along.

Goddess, who had I become? Once, I would've kicked this alpha in the nuts and told him to fuck off before he even attempted to touch me, much less pull me like luggage.

"I can walk," I said, gathering my gumption and wrenching my elbow away.

"Oh, you're feisty tonight. We're gonna have a good time." He opened his coat to show me a glimmer of the three knives he'd brought in.

"I thought you said you didn't have any knives," I said as a slice of fear ripped through me.

"I got some, baby, just for you."

I sighed. Perfect.

We checked our coats and got our rings as we entered the lobby.

"Should we get a drink first?" I asked, wanting to delay whatever he had in mind. I had a feeling that night, he was wanting to make the knife play real, and nothing about that idea thrilled me. In fact, it terrified me.

Aaron cut me a look. Disapproval, I thought. "I suppose. But only one. I'm eager to play tonight."

I shuddered. Not at the change of temperature in the club or the booming of the bass around us but at the thought of being at his mercy.

We had a safe word, but a large part of me thought Aaron wouldn't honor the code, even if I called it out.

I sipped my drink while Aaron pretended, unsuccessfully, not to ogle every omega who passed by.

"Let's go," he said, and pushed my drink away from me even though I'd only taken a few slow sips. On purpose, of course.

We watched an alpha play with his omega. The man being cut cried out in sweet agony as blood rippled from his wounds, but all the time, there was a smile on his face. His alpha asked over and over if this and that was okay and reminded him that he loved him.

"Our turn. Come on."

Again, I let him not so gently lead me to the leather table where I lay down. There was a dungeon monitor in the corner, arms crossed over his chest. He stood in shadow so I couldn't see his eyes, but somehow I felt them on me.

Seeing Aaron take the knife from his pocket, I shivered, and terror gripped my entire body. "I don't think I'm r-ready for this, Aaron," I stuttered.

"Don't be stupid. We've been watching for long enough. It's time to have some real fun."

"No. I changed my mind."

I tried to sit up, but Aaron put his beefy hand right on my chest and pushed me back down. "You'll do as I say, Beale. I mean it. I've waited long enough."

The fuck?

I pushed off the table again, my wolf helping me with a bit of his power.

That's when I felt the crack of his hand against my cheek.

He slapped me.

This fucker slapped me.

"That's enough," a bass voice said.

Chapter Three

Jabez

I was always nervous about knife play. Not that I judged it as bad or wrong, but it had the potential for things to go really bad, which had my healer's heart on edge. In theory, it should be just fine. I watched the scene before me with alertness, although I knew the dom was skilled and would not take things any further than his omega had agreed to. No, it was not something that I chose to indulge in.

Longtime partners had contracts between them that covered aspects of the kink they chose to participate in and any others they might have a future interest in trying out. Often, they went on for pages.

"Did you get authorization for knife play?" Nothing I was seeing here gave me the impression this alpha knew what he was doing. And while every kink under our roof had potential dangers associated with it, few had the potential for a bleed out.

"Obviously I did." The dom whose name I wasn't sure of but who I'd seen here a few times—

and not been impressed by—thrust out his chest and lifted his chin. "Or I wouldn't be here."

I pulled my phone from my pocket. Only owners and authorized staff members could carry phones within the club, all others having checked theirs at the door for obvious reasons. Like the fact that the dom waiting for the knife station was a conservative congressman whose half mask might not be enough to hide his identity should a photo leak onto social media. Even we were not allowed to take pictures, except for very rare circumstances. Like this one. Before pulling up the schedule, I snapped a shot of the wanna-be knife expert as evidence. Memberships did not come cheap, and those who lost theirs for cause would receive no refunds.

"Hey, you're not going to show that to people, are you?" he protested. "I have a reputation to maintain."

"No doubt. This is just for our files." And I could only imagine what his reputation was. "Let me check who has this station at this time." Obviously, I knew, but I still went through the motions. "Yes, it is the gentleman waiting over there who has been authorized for this level of play."

"I have every right to use any station here at any time. I pay for a VIP membership." The dom's attitude was making me want to handle his removal personally, but a glance at the shivering omega standing partially behind him showed me where my priorities lay. I caught the eye of another monitor on duty tonight. Talon. It was a rare situation when two owners were picking up this type of work, but it did happen. Talon, whose love of fire play made him one of the edgy experts, fixed a glare in the direction of the dom. He had been overseeing things a few yards away, but very little got past him. If I hadn't stepped in, I had no doubt he would have.

Without a word spoken between us, my co-owner moved to my side. He looked deceptively casual, but I knew better. Cuffed was a big part of all of us, and we were protective of everything about it, including the members.

"Actually, you must have skimmed the rules because if you had read them carefully, you'd know that is not correct." He was going to be unhappy, was in fact already, and we didn't want to interrupt everyone else's evening any more than we already had if he chose to have a tantrum. I still had to be clear.

"But it doesn't matter whether you read them or not." Talon reached out and took the dom's arm. "I'll have to ask you to come with me."

"I'm in the middle of something here." He tried to shrug free, but the fire master was having none of it, holding him with no apparent strain. "Let me go."

"Afraid I can't do that." Talon started off, towing the dom behind him.

"Where are you trying to take me?" His voice was rising, but another dungeon monitor fell in behind, in the unlikely event that his boss needed backup.

"To the office," Talon informed him. "We need to do some paperwork."

Chapter Four

Beale

"My name is Jabez. Let's go to my office. Do you want a drink? Water?"

My body felt hollow as I forced myself to breathe in and out in a somewhat smooth rhythm, an attempt at self-soothing.

"Um, water. Why? Your office? You're kicking me out?" I asked, not really recognizing my own voice.

"No, of course not. Your name is Beale?"

I nodded. "Yes." There was something about the way he said my name. There was emotion behind it. That one syllable poured from his mouth and all over me. There was more emotion from him in that word than I'd gotten from Aaron in the months we'd dated.

"Beale, I just wanted to talk to you. You're not kicked out. You did nothing wrong."

"Oh. But he...but we...there was commotion."

Jabez laughed. The sound was deep and guttural, born from his chest. "Not the first time there's been commotion in this club and won't be the last. Follow me, please. I have water in my office."

I didn't know much about these kinds of clubs before coming to Cuffed, but of course there were offices here. It was a business, after all. Would dungeon monitors be assigned an office, though?

"Are you sure? I can just leave. I'm okay. I think."

"Your face is reddening. I want to make sure you're fine before I let you go. I'm a healer as well as an owner. Please. Make yourself at home."

An owner? Nothing about his tight T-shirt with the logo and *Monitor* across the chest had told me that.

Inside his office was sparse. A desk with no paperwork scattered. Not even a pen. One computer with three monitors. No family photos or anything else. Not even a landscape. There were no pictures on the pale-gray walls. He was so warm but his office was anything but.

"Thank you. I...you said you are an owner?"

He nodded, waving me to a seat before rounding the desk to take his. My face burned. Maybe it was hot before, but reality and the aftermath were setting in now. "I am. I invested early. Was that...is he your mate? Aaron?"

I laughed, but there was nothing close to comedic about this situation. "No. He's not my mate. My boyfriend. And after tonight, we're no longer even dating. I had a bad feeling about him, and tonight, and I ignored it."

Jabez nodded. "Gut instincts are great, but only if we listen to them. And our animals."

Ah, another shifter. Of course, now that he said it, I'd picked it up by his scent. He was a wolf as well. "That's true. I..."

"Oh, your water." He turned in his chair and got me a cold bottle of water and uncapped it before handing it to me.

I took a drink and sighed. What a night.

"We'd like to refund your membership fee. We don't want you to think we allow this to happen to our members. Of course, you'll keep your membership here."

I scoffed. "I'm not a member. I was his guest."

"Oh. Well, in that case, we'd like to offer you a six-month membership on the house. We want you to come back. I-I want you to come back and enjoy yourself in a safe way. We don't condone that kind of behavior."

"I know that. I've never seen anyone hurt here. At least, not in a way they didn't want."

"Let me get you some ice for your face."

He was up out of the room before I could protest. In his wake, his scent aroused my wolf, bringing him closer to the surface than he had been in a while. He howled inside me at the absence of this alpha I'd just met.

The thing was, after tonight, I didn't trust myself or my wolf to make decisions about dating or mates or men in general.

I should've listened to my instincts.

If Jabez hadn't stepped in, how far would his abuse have gone.

"Here you go." He came back in with an ice pack in hand. "We keep these in stock for other bumps and bruises. All consensual, of course." The tall, broad man sat in the leather chair across from me, and I hissed as he pressed the ice to my face.

"I must look a mess," I said.

"You don't. You're not a mess at all."

"Sure. Sure."

I covered the ice with my hand, and, the moment our skin touched, a thousand alarms went off in my head and my wolf's. This man was something to me. I didn't dare say mate because I'd just met him, and there was a chance this was all a trauma response.

Still, something sparked between us.

He cleared his throat and went back to his chair. I couldn't help but think this big desk was a shield between us. Whether it was protecting me or him, I didn't know.

"Um, thank you for the membership. I don't know if I'll ever come back here, but thank you."

"You're welcome. Here." He reached into the center drawer and pulled out a notebook and a pen. Ah, he did have a pen. "Write down your name so I can access the information from the guest pass and upgrade you."

"Sure." I scribbled the details but more than anything wanted to get out of there. My face throbbed, and my pride was officially broken.

"And I will give you my number so you can reach me if you need to."

My wolf whined for me not to leave.

Jabez meant something to him—to us. I just didn't know what yet.

"I really have to go," I whispered.

"I understand. Let me walk you out."

"Someone might think you did this to me," I joked as we strolled out of his office and down the hallway.

"They know better. I'm a healer. I would never harm an omega." He made sure he had eye contact with me before continuing. "I would never hurt you, Beale. Not in a million years."

"Thank you. I-I'll be fine from here."

"Are you sure? I can call you a ride. Did you drive?"

"No. I'll walk. I walked here. Thanks for everything."

I put my arms into the coat he held out for me and put my phone in my pocket quickly, not wanting him to see that my phone was almost as outdated as my car. "Good night, Jabez."

"Good night, Beale. Sweet dreams."

Chapter Five

Jabez

That omega in the motel occupied the parts of my brain that Beale did not. I was having nightmares about the birth, illustrating how right I was to avoid that aspect of medicine whenever possible, but I had to also think that my strong attraction to the omega was kind of cross-wiring in my thoughts.

It had been a long time since I had any kind of a strong reaction to an omega—since my late mate, in fact. And that was scaring the pants off me. We just met, and I shouldn't be reacting like this to a virtual stranger.

Sitting behind my desk in the executive hallway at Cuffed, I toyed with the electric-blue fidget spinner one of my young patients had given me as a thank-you for helping him through a rare virus. Shifters had so few contagious diseases, and the act of shifting could heal most injuries. But our young were more susceptible to those illnesses and in many cases unable to shift until adolescence.

Fortunately, the little guy made it, and so did the baby I delivered at that motel.

Right after I told him about the home where he and his little one would be able to go and be safe, Rally convulsed. I had to get that baby out of there fast, and surgery would not be my very last option in this place where sanitation was far from optimal. It was bad enough having to use their towels and sheets at all, and what I had in my bag was minimal. If I had to cut the baby out, the father would not be able to shift for at least twenty-four hours, which would give plenty of time for sepsis to set in.

"Ouro," I said to his friend who had just come back in from the bathroom. "I'm going to need you."

I gave him instructions, and we gathered all the towels from the bathroom—both of them— threadbare, though they might be, and I got ready to use everything I had to get that baby safely out of the omega. "Rally." I shook the limp omega's shoulder, a firm jerk that had his buddy ready to protest. "I have to do this, Ouro. I cannot deliver the baby without his help, and yours, okay?"

Ouro was pale, hands shaking, but he went to work to do the things I asked. The first thing was waking the laboring daddy. "Rally, you have to wake up," he said, patting his friend's cheeks. "Or you are going to die. Just when we found somewhere to go off the streets. It's not fair to let your baby pass just because you can't be bothered to open your eyes." He spoke with urgency, close to the other omega's ear, and I let them have at it while I did my job getting ready. I spread the towels under his hips and waited for the next pain, hoping it would not send him into another seizure. It was too late to do anything about elevated blood pressure. Only the birth could save them both.

I massaged his belly, hoping to get the contractions going again. They seemed to have stopped when he convulsed, not terribly uncommon in shifter births according to my mentor. He thought I had a gift with this aspect of our work, and I had been specializing when tragedy sent me on a different trajectory.

How could I possibly mate with anyone else, not that Beale was asking me to. But life was so precious and fragile. If I mated with someone—

anyone—and they got pregnant, it would be my fault if it ended badly. I knew too well what that was like.

Shaking the memories away, I poured a whiskey and sat back to drink it. Not to get drunk. My shifter system required a lot more than one double shot for that, and as a healer, I could be called out at any time to help someone. Incapacitation was not an option.

I picked up my phone and stared at it. As the club healer, it was almost my duty to check in with Beale and make sure he hadn't been suffering any symptoms from his evening at the club. I hated that he might not want to return based on an experience with one bad apple. An apple that would no longer be hanging from any branches on the Cuffed tree.

While the omega's phone rang, once, twice, three times, I tried not to realize how ridiculous my thoughts were. It was better than the despair and fear of the nightmares I had.

"Hello." His voice sounded good.

"Hi, Beale. This is Jabez." Which of course he knew, since we'd exchanged numbers in the phones. "Just checking in to see how you're doing."

"That's nice of you," he said.

I waited for more, but it was quiet on the other end. "Well, after your experience here, I was concerned. I'm the healer, after all."

"Yes, you mentioned that." Another moment of silence, followed by, "But I'm perfectly fine, really." Which I might have believed if his voice hadn't cracked on the word fine. He was lying to me. Which tensed every muscle in my body.

"Are you sure?" I toyed with the pen that had been on my desk since I last saw him. "Because it's fine to admit if you're not."

"No, I am."

"All right, then. That was all I needed to hear. Have a good evening."

He said goodbye and disconnected, and all I could think of was another lie that had led to tragedy. No matter how much I was attracted to this omega, or concerned for him, I had to step back. I'd decided long ago not to get involved again. And if I did, it wouldn't be with someone who was dishonest about their feelings or their health. Not again.

Chapter Six

Beale

A few days later, I still couldn't get Jabez off my mind. The way he spoke. He cared for me more in one night than anyone ever had in my life.

He smelled like brown sugar and vanilla. I'd even baked some cookies to try and emulate the scent, but they didn't come close to him.

My face healed quickly, the bruises fading as soon as I shifted, but the wounds of that night stuck with me. I blamed myself at first. If I'd called out the safe word sooner. Not given Aaron the wrong idea about how far I wanted to go.

No way. None of what happened that night was my fault. None of it. A submissive, an omega, like me, put their full trust into the dom, the alpha. He violated that trust. The submissive made the calls. The alpha only did what he was given permission to do.

From here on out, I would go with my gut instinct.

Then again, if I had, I might not have met Jabez.

His eyes and touch haunted my dreams. I wanted to go back there, with my new free membership, and visit him. See what he was into. I would bet anything he wouldn't hurt a fly. Maybe he was into feather play or something else more sensual.

I still didn't know all the ins and outs of people's preferences. Aaron had only wanted to watch the exhibits that included pain and blood.

I would be safe at Cuffed. Not only had they kicked Aaron out of the club, but they had banned him for life.

Would it be weird to go there just to see him? His scent seemed to indicate he was unmated, but I hadn't asked. Didn't seem like the right place or time.

Still, I wanted to know.

And now wasn't the right time for me either. I needed to heal. What happened with Aaron was not the root issue. I had to believe I was worth more than someone who would abuse me in any way. I had to gain enough self-confidence and security not to fall for anyone's bullshit again.

Still, my fantasies steered toward Jabez.

I wanted him in my bed and in my life.

Being alone sucked, but I had to learn to be good with myself before I could be good with someone else.

At least, that's what the self-help books touted. I'd been binging on them this week. Even before that.

After a long day, I needed a bite to eat. Fast food gave me the ick lately, and so did diner food. I wanted a real meal, but cooking was not my forte.

"Take yourself out to dinner. That's what one of the books said," I told myself in the mirror. I'd had some sleepless nights since Aaron. Not because of him calling me, at least. As soon as I got home that night, I'd blocked him in all the places. My phone. My socials. Everything. Not that I thought he would try to get in contact with me. I'd ruined his good time.

Bastard.

I showered and changed clothes. The nights were still a bit chilly, so I opted for a long-sleeve button-down shirt with a sweater on top and my nicest jeans. There was a restaurant right down the street that I'd been wanting to try for a while but for one reason or another hadn't gone to. I'd passed it one night, and the food smelled incredible.

I'd never taken myself out on a date. There was a first time for everything.

"Table for two?" the female at the hostess stand asked as I walked in a few minutes later.

"No. One, please." *Gulp*.

"Perfect. Right this way."

She showed me to a small round table right in the middle of the restaurant. She might as well have put a sign on me and a glass case since I felt like a museum exhibit. I could feel everyone staring, judging, wondering about the pathetic guy who didn't even have a friend, much less a date to eat with. I thought about bolting. Fast food wasn't that horrible, and I made a mean egg sandwich in a pinch.

"Anything to drink?" The waiter placed my menu in front of me. First mistake. I should've looked at the menu before I came so I would already know what I wanted.

"Just water, please."

He nodded. "Would you like to hear about the specials?"

Sweat beaded up along my brow and trickled down the back of my neck. Tingles broke out along my arms, and my leg bounced.

I tugged at my collar, wishing I hadn't worn a sweater.

Why was it so hot in here?

"No. No specials. Thank you."

"Sir, are you all right?" he asked, bending down a bit to whisper.

"I'll be fine. Water. Please."

The chatter from the other diners got louder until the separate voices blended into a roar in my ears. I gripped the edge of the table for some kind of stability, but even that didn't help.

Closing my eyes, I took a long deep breath, but that only made my heart stutter harder.

This was all a bad idea.

Taking myself out.

The night with Aaron.

Trying to be alone.

If only I had something or someone to ground me.

Chapter Seven

Jabez

I didn't have a real problem with eating alone because as a healer, my schedule could be so erratic that I could find myself eating breakfast when others were having dinner or vice versa. Even though I tried to leave the birthings to other healers and midwives, attending to illnesses and injuries did not take place only during regular business hours. And often, I had just a little while between calls, not nearly long enough to go home and prepare a full meal. So, it was either get used to sitting alone in restaurants or go hungry.

And my wolf and I did not like going hungry.

So while I preferred eating with friends or other healers or even business associates, I found myself alone in restaurants far too often. And I had come up with a system to make sure my meals were as relaxing and nourishing as possible. First, I insisted on a booth or at least a table out of the way. Nothing worse than being stuck in the middle of noisy diners and staff constantly passing by when I'd been up for thirty-six hours and wasn't going to get to sleep anytime soon. I needed to use my break to restore my energy to be there for my patients.

Another thing was what I chose to eat. It was entirely too easy in restaurants to eat heavy food, or fried, or just too much salt or sugar. My wolf craved meat, of course, so I never cut back on that, choosing high protein most of the time and saving the heavy starches for special treats. And dessert, well, I just didn't have the time or energy to weight myself down with that. But I did have a love for all things dark chocolate.

However, tonight, I had decided to indulge in one of my favorite meals. And that meant going to my favorite restaurant. An out-of-the-way steakhouse, it always managed to be busy yet always managed to get me one of the booths I preferred even without a reservation. Just like any other physician, my healer status granted me that privilege. Mostly, the job was hard and grueling and, even avoiding my Achilles of birthing, could emotionally take a toll.

"Healer Jabez, lovely to see you tonight." Betsy, a cougar shifter, picked up a menu and waved it. "I don't suppose you need this?"

"No, but you may be surprised at what I order." I followed her up a flight of five steps to a booth in the back section, a place as quiet and secluded as possible in this popular restaurant.

"I'm intrigued." She grinned. "I hope that includes dessert."

"It might, but"—I crooked a finger, inviting her to lean close—"I am going to have some of those potatoes au gratin your mate creates."

She fake gasped. "But you claim they can clog even the arteries of a shifter."

"What is life without its little treats."

"Agreed." I leaned back in my seat and let my tense shoulder muscles relax as she stepped away. Betsy and her mate had opened this place a couple of years earlier, and they drew a mixed clientele of shifters and humans and some people who did not fit into either category. It was one of the reasons I enjoyed coming here and watching all the activity that went on. I just didn't want to be in the middle of it. My current perch allowed quite a view of all the goings-on.

My server, Eduardo, brought me a drink without my having to ask. I kept a bottle in the bar here, on the top shelf, for a fee I considered

well worth it to enjoy my preferred whiskey. "And
what will you have tonight, Healer? Steak and
salad? No dressing?"

"No. I would like bleu cheese on the salad,
yes on the steak, but for a side..."

He grinned at me. "The potatoes."

"And don't skimp on the bread." I usually
didn't have them bring any, but tonight, I was
just in the mood for all the tasty things."

"It's one of those days. Shall I have the chef
start a souffle for you?"

"Why not?" I glanced around the room,
looking to see if any of my patients were there to
notice their healer eating everything he
recommended they go light on. Shifter
metabolisms were amazing, but that didn't mean
we couldn't take care to feel our very best. "Bring
it all."

He left for a moment and returned with a
basket piled high with mini baguettes they were
known for. Betsy's other mate not only operated a
successful Parisian-style bakery down the street,
but he provided all the bread products and many
of the dessert served at the family steakhouse.

And, even better, he sent the risen loaves here to be baked, so the one I tore open and slathered with softened butter was still warm. As I sank my teeth into its goodness, crisp on the outside and tender within, I congratulated myself on resisting so often and decided that some things were worth not skipping. Being a healer sometimes made me too rigid.

I settled in to people watch.

Unless I told them I was in a hurry, the staff did not rush me, and I had finished my drink and half of the bread by the time my salad arrived. Like everything else here, it was fresh and would be delicious, especially with the creamy chunks of bleu cheese scattered over the crisp greens and baby vegetables. They sourced locally where possible, too, which I appreciated. Tonight, there seemed to be mostly humans here, all chattering away about this and that and creating a low hum of noise. A couple near the front were arguing about money, and three men in suits were discussing business.

But then my gaze lit on a familiar face, my fork landed next to my plate, and I was on my feet and crossing the room before I had time to consider whether it was a good idea.

Mate.

Don't you dare start that. We already had a mate, and he's dead.

Mate. Stubborn wolf.

Chapter Eight

Beale

I was losing it. Right there in the damned restaurant. I just had to come here. Bring myself on a date.

What a stupid idea.

Sweat trickled down the length of my spine as I tried to read the menu. There was a small stain on the parchment-like paper, and I focused on it with every ounce of presence I had left while I planned my exit.

I looked up, desperate for that water the waiter promised me.

That's when I saw him.

Jabez. I shook my head, thinking I was daydreaming. Either that, or I had passed out right there at the table. I reached down and pinched at the side of my thigh, trying to wake myself before someone else had to. The last thing I needed or wanted was more embarrassment. Hissing at the pinch, I realized I wasn't dreaming or passed out.

He was here. At this place. His eyes were on me as he came closer.

My wolf let out a long, low howl. I didn't recognize that noise from him.

"Jabez," I choked out, mentally cursing the waiter for failing to bring me water.

"Beale, I thought that was you. Are you alone? Expecting someone?" His hand touched my shoulder and instantly, the world stopped spinning and I was able to breathe again.

"No. I'm here. Dating myself. Taking myself out on a date." It sounded as lame out loud as it did in my head. Great.

"Oh, and here I was going to ask you to join me for dinner."

"You're eating here?" Boy, I was a genius tonight.

"I am. I hate to eat alone though. When I saw you across the room, I thought you might want to join me. But if you're having a good time alone..."

"No." I stood, nearly toppling the chair over. "I'm not. I would love to join you."

"Excellent. I have a booth over there. Not so many prying eyes."

Did he know how much that bothered me? Sitting in the middle of the room with their stares drilling holes into my back?

We walked over to the booth together. It took everything in me not to reach out and hold his hand. He had a presence. The way he walked. Talked. Owned the room. I'd touched him momentarily the other night, but I couldn't help but wonder what it would be like to sink into his embrace. To melt into his body. Let him hold me. Make me safe again.

"Please, sit." I sat down and he did the same. One flick of his fingers had the same waiter rushing over to fill a pitcher full of ice water and place a new glass in front of me. "Water?" The alpha was a mind reader. I drained the glass in seconds, but he didn't flinch.

I wondered for a second what his kink was. Something where he was in control, no doubt. Firm hand. Steady breaths. Goddess, he turned me on. It was a good thing we were sitting on opposite sides of a booth.

"I was surprised it was so chilly tonight," he said. "May I order for you? I come here a lot. Unless you had something in mind."

"Please do. Thank you. I've never been here before."

Another flick of his fingers had the waiter returning. "Something else, Healer?" He blinked a little too much.

"Yes. Double my order, please. My new friend is hungry. Bring them out at the same time—"

"Oh, you don't have to do that," I interrupted. "Really. You can bring his food out as soon as it's ready."

"At the same time," he told the waiter who soon returned with our meals.

"It was chilly the other night. When I was at the club." He had started a conversation about the weather so I followed. Not what I wanted to talk about with him but it would do.

Jabez nodded. "You never know with spring." We talked about other things while waiting for the food. Our favorite seasons. My favorite dessert. He told me he skipped dessert more often than not but partook of a single square of dark chocolate at night.

I could imagine this gentle giant sitting in his bed, naked, covered only by a sheet from the waist down, gently putting a square of luscious chocolate past those full lips.

"Beale?" he asked. "Did you hear me?"

Shit. I'd been fantasizing about him again. Right here. I had to get myself together.

"I'm sorry. I didn't."

He chuckled low and deep, doing nothing to weaken my raging hard-on. "Are you enjoying the food?"

He'd ordered us steak and potatoes au gratin. Nothing I would've gotten for myself but... "It's incredible."

"That's good to hear."

The night dwindled and once we were done with our meal, Jabez put his napkin on the table. "I have to get to work but tonight was lovely."

"It was. Thank you for not making me eat alone."

"Funny. I was going to say the same thing to you. Next time you want to go out to dinner or lunch or breakfast or anything else, call me. I'm always up for a good meal with excellent company."

"Okay."

He paid the check after a little protest from me.

47

Lorelei M. Hart

"I have one condition," I said as he got up to leave.

"Name it, omega."

The word rolled over me like warm honey. "You let me pick up the bill next time."

Jabez bent down, pressing his lips to my earlobe. "Of course, Beale. Until next time."

Chapter Nine

Jabez

A couple of days had passed since I had dinner with the omega. I told myself that I should not contact him, allowing him to do so if he chose. He'd insisted that the next time we ate, it would be his turn to pay, and although I did not want him to, if it meant I had the opportunity to see him again, I'd bite the bullet and allow him to do so.

As I dressed for the evening in the private bathroom off my office, I tried to think of a place to suggest, somewhere inexpensive enough not to tax his budget but nice enough not to insult him. His clothing was neat and clean but not expensive, and I saw no reason to make him spend dollars he couldn't afford just to make up to me for a meal whose cost I barely noticed.

I wondered how I had never noticed him at the club before the night I banished his former wanna-be dom, but truth was, I had not spent many evenings at Cuffed in the past few months. My work had taken up a great deal of time, and I'd been out of town for a while at a healers' retreat. One thing and another had me too busy to be where I preferred.

And this was something I was determined to change.

Not just because Beale might be there. Or rather not only for that reason. I was supposed to be the healer on staff, and although I did trainings with all our employees on how to handle any accidental—and they'd be better be accidental—injuries, nobody was better prepared to do that job. My fellow owners counted on me to be there and had been very understanding when I was not.

On this night, I had agreed to get out my favorite toys and offer all comers a chance to experience something that might be new to them. Not many people understood the violet wand and its erotic and healing properties. I'd been to one too many conferences where someone was selling the devices and loading down beginners with the heavy-duty electromechanical types that would give "the ultimate" erotic sensations. Some of these salesmen even guaranteed their customers orgasms like they'd never dreamed possible.

Returning to my office, I opened the antique chest where I kept all my wands and attachments. It had once been in a sea captain's cabin, traveling all over the world, according to the antique dealer who sold it to me, and I wasn't sure that was true. But it was very old and still had that amazing wood smell I loved whenever I pulled out a drawer or opened one of its little doors.

When I scened, especially with an experienced omega, I might bring out the serious devices, but for a demonstration, like tonight, where anyone was allowed to participate? Solid state all the way. I lifted out the case I would bring with me onto the main floor and filled it with all the attachments I thought I might like to use with those who cared to try.

Nothing I had here was dangerous, in theory, but I would keep control of it at all times because anything could cause harm in careless or inexperienced hands.

"You about ready?" One of the DMs for the night rapped on my open office door. "We've had several people ask if you were going to 'really' demo tonight."

"Can't blame them." I'd had to cancel three times due to medical emergencies requiring my attention. My mentor had told me that I could expect a light schedule as a pack healer, but he'd never imagined what it would be like in the big city where I not only had a full practice but the additional duties of Cuffed. I needed to look into taking on an apprentice soon so they could learn in time to be of help before I totally burned out. "Be there in two."

"Okay, boss." He cast me a sympathetic smile. As well as a paid staff member here, Julio was an EMT. "I know what it's like to be needed by someone."

"Julio, have you ever considered giving up your work with humans?"

His eyes widened. "Why? What have you heard?"

I silently cursed myself. The prejudice against shifters in some human quarters could be extreme. Many still thought we were the stuff of romance novels, but among those who did acknowledge us as sharers of the Earth with them, a small percentage didn't want us to continue to do that. Or at least not in their

52

backyard, so to speak. "Nothing. I am going to be looking for an apprentice soon. My practice is more than I can comfortably handle, and you're already helping out here with your medical skills."

"And you would consider me?" The coyote shifter was an excellent dungeon monitor, careful and vigilant, and he'd bandaged nearly as many boo-boos as I had. "I don't know what to say."

"Say you'll think about it. It's a big decision, and it doesn't pay much at first."

"But I—"

"Think!" I ordered, chuckling to ease any sting as I guided him out the door. "Go make sure the lighting is set up for my demo. Last time, my remote didn't work, and I couldn't turn it on and off as needed. It ruined the whole effect."

"On it." He dug in his heels for just a moment. "But I am most likely going to take you up on your offer. My omega dad always wanted me to be a 'real' healer."

"I'd say you do a fair amount of real healing every day, but I understand. He probably would feel more comfortable with you working more with shifters."

Lorelei M. Hart

"There is prejudice on both sides," he agreed. "Not only the humans."

After he headed out, I finished loading my case and followed. The club was packed, and there were more people hovering around my station than would be there by chance. They expected a show, but first, they were going to get a lecture.

Chapter Ten

Beale

Jabez is not only haunting my dreams, but my every waking thought now. He had picked up all my pieces and put them back together twice—once at the club and then at the restaurant.

I'd typed out a text to him over a dozen times only to delete. I didn't send a single one.

When I was walking in the coffee shop, I swore I'd seen him walking by the window or getting in line, but it wasn't him. Only my imagination.

I sat down the next night with my phone in my hands, wondering how bold I could be. We did have a loose arrangement where I told him that I wanted to treat him to a meal after everything he'd done for me.

While he hadn't said a single word about my distress the night at the restaurant, I had a feeling he knew. He saw that I was struggling to keep myself together and came over to help me—again.

He always seemed to show up exactly when I needed him.

Being a barista barely paid my rent. I didn't have a lot of extra money to take him somewhere fancy or anywhere at all. As it was, I had intended to pay for my night out with one of my credit cards. It was an exception to my rules for life, since I could do that, but I hated running up debt.

I would consider it worthwhile to charge a meal for this alpha, so I needed to come up with a place. Sure, I'd had dinner with Jabez at a semi-fancy restaurant, but I wanted to bring him somewhere fancy. Somewhere we could have a nice sit-down dinner.

I didn't even own anything to wear for that.

I was pitching above my league with Jabez. He was an owner of a club and a healer.

Hell, there was a chance that all of our interactions had been simply out of pity.

Still, something in me wanted to take a chance. On him. On us.

Since dating Aaron, I'd gotten to know some of the omegas at the club. Maybe they could suggest a restaurant where they had been with their alphas.

They were my only friends. Sure, I had some acquaintances at the coffee shop, but we didn't socialize outside of work hours. They had families and lives. They had never invited me out, and Aaron would not have approved of my going even if they had.

I got dressed for Cuffed after a shower and a quick bite. Cheese and crackers, since I had to watch my pennies until payday and the cupboards were growing bare. Wrapping my coat around myself, I braved the chill of the night and arrived at Cuffed right as it opened.

Floods of people were coming in, all with dates or mates.

I wished Jabez were with me. Letting me nestle into his warmth and strength. Sure, I'd been to the club before, but never alone.

I gave the person at the front desk my name, and he took my phone and locked it up then told me to enjoy my night. I left my coat and wallet in a locker and moved on to the main floor.

Passing on getting a drink, which would take money I did not have, I looked around, wanting to take in some of the activity at the various stations, this time without Aaron balking or huffing out his disapproval over my shoulder. He only liked the knife stuff.

At the first station I came to, an omega was strapped to a leather-covered bench, ass thrust up into the air while his alpha spanked his pale skin to rosy red.

I might want to explore that. Of course, I'd have to have someone to try it with. My mind immediately went to Jabez. There was no one else I trusted. He would never harm me. I believed that with my whole heart.

The beast inside me called out for him, although I hadn't seen him anywhere. Damn it. Maybe I should've texted to ask if he was here before coming.

A sinking feeling suddenly made me sick to my stomach. He could be mated. Perhaps he was dating someone or had a boyfriend. An omega of his own. Maybe I'd read all the signs wrong. He was only being nice. Taking pity on me.

This was a mistake.

Still, I wandered the club, hoping to see him. None of the omegas I knew were around tonight.

"There he is," someone whispered, not to me, but it garnered my attention all the same.

"Who?" another one asked.

"Jabez. Goddess, he has the violet wands."

Swallowing the boulder now lodged in my throat, I turned to where they stared.

That's when I saw him. He had all black on. Black button-down shirt, cuffs rolled up to his elbows. Black pants. He stood in a pool of light, and all eyes were on him.

He stopped what he was doing and looked to the side. Not completely over his shoulder but as though he could feel me there—near.

I hoped he could. Not only did I want to see what he was doing, whatever it was, I wanted him to do it to me.

Chapter Eleven

Jabez

I had just set up my station when I sensed him. Somewhere in the crowd pressing in around me, my omega. The omega, rather. He was here somewhere. My wolf rumbled in my chest, demanding we find him immediately and haul him off to our den. *Mate. Mark. Mine.*

My head swiveled, eyes searching for the source of the scent making my nostrils twitch. Where? I straightened up and even rose a bit off my heels, but wherever he was, there were too many people around. Which set my wolf off even more—he did not like our omega surrounded by potential enemies—his word, not mine—when we were not in direct line of sight or, even better, touching him.

Then, a couple of people moved aside, and there he was. Making no effort to move forward or catch my attention. But he had not only come to the club but also found his way to my demo. Which had not quite begun, and suddenly my idea of allowing everyone to experience the wand faded into the background.

Did he—would he like to try out electrical play? Only one way I could think of to find out without putting him in the spotlight if he didn't want it.

So, I launched into my opening spiel, giving the basics of how the wand worked, the various types, and something about the attachments.

"There are both erotic and health applications of this device going back a century or more. I could go on for hours about how it can be used by a healer in his medical practice, but I have a feeling most of you would rather read up on that in your own time. Am I correct in your preference to hear about the erotic aspects of my favorite toys?"

The spatter of applause and laughter confirmed what I'd already known to be true.

"Well, then, I guess we'd better get started. But I can't do this alone."

The laughter stilled, and heat darkened more than one pair of eyes. I had done this demo or a version of it with many of the omegas in the group, and there were some passionate adherents as well as others who would probably love to have the electricity nibble at their nerve endings. But tonight, if he was willing, I would only play with one particular omega tonight—if he was willing. But with a gathering ready to observe, there must be an element of showmanship. If I could, I'd grab his hand and drag him off somewhere private. I had a bit of exhibitionist in me, but the first time scening with my omega? No. Not my omega. This omega.

"Any volunteers?"

Hands shot up, more than a dozen, all around Beale, who seemed locked in a dream, his gaze fixed on me but arm relentlessly at his side. If he did not volunteer, I would have to go back to my original idea, hoping that after he saw a few others participate, he would be emboldened to give it a shot.

He might not like electrical play; it wasn't everyone's cup of tea. And that was not a deal-breaker for me. Sure, it was my favorite toy, but I also enjoyed other kinks. I knew he wasn't into knives, fortunately, because it was not ever going to be my thing. If he liked fire, I'd do some more work with Talon and up my skills. Spanking, I enjoyed. Wax...there were so many kinks, and I was very interested in learning which he might like. The fact he'd been here before, more than a few times according to some of my employees, meant he must have something he wanted or needed from kink.

Chancing it all, I took the steps, one, two, three, to arrive in front of him and held out my hand. "How about you?"

"He didn't have his hand up," another omega, who was a big fan of the wand, protested. "Why him?"

I pivoted to take in the argumentative one and fixed them with a narrow-eyed stare. He melted back into the crowd, leaving me to return my attention to Beale. My hand was still extended. "Omega? Are you interested?"

"Yes...sir," he whispered, his voice so low even my shifter hearing barely managed to catch it. "Please."

He laid his hand in mine and I closed my fingers over it, the connection sending more electricity up my arm than any wand ever could. "All right, then." I led him to the chair in the middle of the station, right under the light from high above. Leaning close, I whispered, "For this evening, we will use the red, yellow, green safe

64

words." The club used the standard definitions of go, slow down, and stop, and anyone who participated in any scene should know that.

He nodded. "I understand."

"This is just a demo, so I won't be doing anything crazy. Have you ever done a wand scene before?"

"No, sir," he murmured. "But I've wanted to."

"Then this is both of our lucky days." I released his hand and stepped back. "I will ask for quiet during this demonstration, so everyone can hear." There was music, of course. Always. But our DJ kept it low enough for the real business of Cuffed to be heard. Cries of pain and ecstasy, the crack of the whip, slap of a hard palm on a vulnerable bare bottom, and, of course, the crackle and snap of electricity were our real sound tracks. "Would you mind taking off your shirt, omega?"

I spoke more than I actually used the devices, sensing nerves from the omega, and wanting our first real intimacy to be just the two of us. But even the glass tip lightly run up his arm had him shivering, his nipples hard pebbles and a bulge straining his zipper. Oh yeah. We were going to have a good time getting to know one another.

While speaking to the watchers, I also whispered low in the omega's ear. Words of praise, telling him how sweet he was, how responsive, and how hard he made me.

Finally, I clicked the light off and our area was shadowy enough for the trails of sparks over the omega's skin to create a display drawing *oohs* and *aahs*.

"So, that's how the violet wand works, or at least a beginner's class. I hope you've all learned something and enjoyed yourselves."

I certainly had.

Chapter Twelve

Beale

My skin, no, my entire body, still buzzed from the experience with Jabez.

His patience. The slow torture. The zips and buzzes of the electricity along the surface of my skin still resounded through my veins, reminding me of what we'd done.

I fucking knew knives weren't my thing.

My preference was whatever wand Jabez wielded.

"Please tell me you brought a coat," the alpha whispered in my ear.

"I did. I left it in a locker."

The last thing I wanted to do was be out of this alpha's presence, but the weight of everything that happened tonight had exhausted me in a strange, delicious way. The need to curl up in his embrace pulsed stronger than ever.

"Good, sweet omega. I'm glad you take care of yourself."

"Thanks," I muttered, not really knowing how to respond to that. Hearing his praise added a layer of sweetness to him and made my knees weak.

He held out his hand for the key to the locker, retrieved my coat, and put it on me as he had before and reached into his pocket, retrieving a long, finely woven red scarf. I didn't even know how it fit into those tight pants. "This is mine." He folded it around my neck and tucked it into the collar of my coat. "It will keep you warm on your drive home."

"Oh, I walked, so even better."

Jabez cocked his head, regarding me with a stare I didn't recognize. Of course, I barely knew the man. But damn, I wanted to. Wanted to see the look in his eyes as he hovered above my body, fucking me in long, languid strokes. To see his ruffled hair first thing in the morning. I'd do anything to learn more about him.

"You walked here? I... It's not safe for you to walk back alone." He looked behind him, conflicted. He was an owner here. He had work to do. Things to handle. Plus, he was a healer. People needed him.

I bet no one on earth needed him more in this moment than I did, though. But I couldn't let my own needs surpass those of all the others.

"I'm a big boy," I said, laughing.

He stroked my cheek with his knuckles. "No boy. You are quite the man. I wish I could walk you home myself, but I have things to do here."

"It's okay. How about I text you when I get home."

"Why didn't you drive? You have valet privileges."

Shrugging one shoulder, for a blip of a second, I considered lying. "I have an old car. It barely gets me to work. I give the old girl a rest when I can. Besides, I like to walk at night."

"Would you let me get you a ride?" He stepped closer to me, pinning me against the nearest wall. Bass pounded all around us, and people's conversations roared and moved in waves.

"It's not necessary."

He made a low sound deep in his throat. "How about this? It would give me great pleasure to see that you're taken home safely, omega."

Mine. Omega mine. I would've done just about anything in that moment to hear that.

"Well, I don't want to deny you any pleasure, alpha. Sure. But, I owe you twice."

He ordered a ride on an app on his phone and then moved us outside with his hand on the small of my back. "You don't owe me anything, Beale. I would love that dinner with you though. How about somewhere not so fancy? I'm a simple man. In fact, I prefer simple."

My heart sank. He could probably tell I didn't have a lot of money.

"How about Friday night? I'm off of work. Oh, but Cuffed is probably pretty busy that night, right?"

"I'm actually free on Friday. I'd love to go to dinner with you. What time?"

We decided on seven, and he insisted on picking me up.

"Text me when you get home, please," he asked again.

"Of course." I opened the door to the car to get in, but he shut it as I turned.

"There's something I've been wanting to do all night, Beale. All day. Ever since the first time I saw you."

"We did a lot tonight," I said, giggling.

70

"Can I kiss you, omega?" he asked, brushing some of my hair from my face.

"Please," I whined and swayed into his hold. Where I'd wanted to be so badly.

He bent ever so slightly and his full lips pressed against mine. I stepped back, but he caught me, moving me to press against his body. It was a simple kiss. No tongue. No open mouth. No moaning.

Still, I was hotter than I'd ever been. My cock punched against the front of my pants, begging to be freed.

"Oh," I said as he pulled away.

"You're so sexy, Beale. I can't wait until Friday night. Go on and go home before I change my mind."

Chapter Thirteen

Jabez

Friday took forever to arrive. Normally, I would have been at the club that night, but I didn't have any particular assignments, so I wasn't strictly lying and would have no problem not being there. While I had looked forward to an evening hanging out at the club, I was much more excited about spending an evening getting to know Beale. My wolf was 100 percent sure he was our omega despite the fact that I told him we'd already had one. Fate would not be so kind as to bestow a second true mate on us, especially after I let the first one die on my watch.

It was more than survivor's guilt that motivated my avoidance of any kind of serious future relationships. I should have known something was wrong. I lived with that omega for a few years, slept with him every night I wasn't on duty during my training, knew his body better than my own, and yet, I didn't recognize his state of health until it was too late?

I almost stopped practicing at that point, doubtful of my abilities, despite my mentor's insistence that there was no way I could have known. And he pointed out all the people who I'd saved with the skills I'd gained. My omega had deliberately kept something important from me, something he'd known nearly his whole life. A weakness that would probably never have been an issue had he obeyed his healer's instructions and avoided pregnancy.

It was so rare, my mentor had never seen it in all his decades in practice, although he had read about it. And of course, I'd never asked why he was on birth control when we met. It seemed logical enough not to want to get pregnant before finding his true mate. I also never asked if there was any life-threatening reason not to get pregnant. What alpha would even think to ask that? As my mentor put it to me, "The lie of omission killed him."

So I continued as a healer, learning everything I could about any condition that could affect a shifter, both common and rare. Became an expert to the point I traveled several times a year to speak on the subject. Also, that contributed to the long hours I put in. And I was very glad to be consulted. If I could spare one omega what happened to mine, one alpha the loss of his mate, or vice versa, I was all there for it.

Beale, I'd noticed, would tell white lies to avoid upsetting people, and that was something we'd have to deal with. I still wasn't sure I could give myself fully to another mate, if indeed Fate had bestowed one upon us. But one thing I could do was have a fun evening out with Beale. Dinner and maybe a shift after?

I pulled up in front of his apartment building to find him reaching for something inside a car that looked even worse than he'd described. The tires weren't bald, but they weren't far from it. I wanted to have them replaced, but I'd probably already insulted him by suggesting the less expensive place for dinner. One thing at a time.

If he was my omega, he'd have to learn that money didn't matter. I had more than him, and what I had would be spent in the best way for us both. If...so many ifs.

I parked behind the beat-up sedan and got out of the car. "Hi."

Beale quickly closed the car door and took a step back as if he could disassociate himself from his mode of transportation. No wonder he walked most places. Forget replacing the tires. The whole thing looked like it would fall apart if someone sneezed too close to it. I hadn't seen a bumper held on with baling wire since I left the pack. Where did you even find baling wire in the city? "Hello, sir. I was just getting, I mean, I left my wallet in here earlier."

"Not good, huh?" Not very responsible. "Do you usually leave it there?"

"No, it fell out of my pocket earlier, and I was afraid I'd lost it."

"I see. Glad you found it." I took his hand and linked our fingers. "Do you need to go back inside for anything?"

"No. I'm ready to go." He was wearing a light jacket this evening, but it wasn't nearly as cold as it had been lately, so he should be fine. "I've been looking forward to this evening all week."

"Me too." I leaned in and brushed a soft kiss over his warm lips. "And to that."

He let out a sigh. "Yes, sir."

"I think we can leave 'sir' in the club or if we scene somewhere else. For now, Jabez is good."

"Okay, Jabez."

I helped him into the car and reached across to pull his seat belt into place, clicked it closed. "There you go. All safe and sound. Let's go eat dinner. I'm starving. I skipped lunch, in fact."

"Me too," he said then snapped his lips closed as if it had been a big admission.

Was he short on food? I might not be able to do much about his car yet, but I would not stand for him going hungry. My wolf growled so loud, I drew a startled gaze from the omega.

"Is your wolf mad?"

"Only because he doesn't want you to miss a meal."

"I won't if you won't," he sassed then gulped.

I couldn't suppress my chuckle even if I had wanted to. "That's a deal I will hold you to."

His smile made my heart beat harder and louder. And my wolf settled down, although he was still not happy about the hungry-omega thing. We'd feed him as soon as possible, no matter who paid for it.

We arrived at the little bistro I had picked out and found street parking, but no sooner were we walking into the place than my phone buzzed. Oh hell. I read the screen and sighed. "Omega, I have to go to work. There was another healer covering for me, in case of emergency, but he fell and broke his leg an hour ago." That would put him out of commission for at least the night, depending on how bad it was. Shifting would help, but it could only heal so much so fast.

"Is it him you need to take care of?"

"No, he's handling it, but I have one of those emergencies he was supposed to cover—and now I have to do it. Let me take you home first, though." I squeezed his hand. "We can drive through somewhere on the way and get you dinner."

Chapter Fourteen

Beale

On the way to the alpha's car, I stopped walking and tugged on his hand. "Jabez, if someone needs you at the hospital, you need to be there right away, right? Why don't you go on, and I can get a ride. Every second counts."

"I'm not ready to let you go," he said. "I can get you that burger or whatever you like then drop you off on the way. It won't take that long. There are other healers at the hospital."

Sweet alpha. I wanted to go on this date, but I'd never be able to live with myself if someone didn't get the treatment they needed all because I was selfish and wanted this alpha to myself. "I have an idea, but let's get walking again."

He nodded. "What's the idea?"

"I'll come with you and wait in the car. I'm not ready for this date to end either. I want more time with you. I've become greedy."

He chuckled and opened the door for me. He got in the driver's side and turned the car on. "Are you sure? It might be hours. I don't even know what's going on with the patient. There might be tests and procedures. Hell, I might be there all night."

As he pulled out of the parking spot, his anxiety pulsed between us. Just like the other night at the club, the alpha, my alpha, was torn between those who needed him and his responsibilities and me. Flattering, sure, but I hated that he had to choose.

"I don't care. I'll take a nap or play on my phone in the car."

"A parking lot isn't the safest place," he grumbled.

"I'll be fine, Jabez. I will."

Growling, he gripped my hand tighter. "Omega, I swear, every time you say my name, my wolf goes nuts. It's like you're speaking directly to him."

I looked out the passenger window, sure I was blushing like a teenager. "I bet he's beautiful."

"He's eager to see your wolf as well."

I turned back, watching him as he drove. He took the turns with such care and ease, driving the car with control. His clenched jaw made me wonder if he was tense because of the emergency or because of me. Selfishly, I hoped it was me.

A few miles later, we arrived at the hospital. It was small in comparison to the big campuses of most human facilities, and nothing about it announced that it was anything more than a small private hospital with no ER. Of course, they had emergency accommodations, but that kept humans from showing up for services, he'd explained. Jabez reached for the placard in his glove box and retrieved it, brushing my thigh. He glanced at me with darkened eyes as he put the piece of plastic on the rearview mirror. Yeah, he knew the effect he had on me.

"I have a better idea," he said. "But only if you agree. I don't like the idea of you staying in this parking lot alone. There are security guards, and I doubt anything would happen, but I wouldn't be able to focus on my patient, knowing there was even a slight chance you were in danger here."

"What's the idea?" I asked as he had earlier.

"How about you stay in my office while I work? I have a couch in there. Snacks in the drawer. No one will bother you."

"Are you sure? That's not against some rules?"

"Not at all."

He came over to open my door, and we walked hand in hand into the hospital. The security guard gave me a sticker ID to put on my jacket. We speed-walked to the elevator and in minutes were in his office. He had a nameplate on his door and everything.

Goddess, I was out of my league. This man was a healer and a successful businessman with omegas probably lining up to be with him. Strike probably. There were tons of omegas who watched him at the club with desire in their eyes.

"Come in. Please. Make yourself at home."

The office was all clean lines and no extraneous items, just like his office at the club. The only frames on the walls held his accolades from various trainings and some honors from the hospital itself.

"I'm going to change." Jabez went into the bathroom while I read over his achievements. The alpha was talented in all ways. From what I could tell, he was as close to perfect as I could imagine anyone getting.

That only begged the question louder. Why in the world was an alpha like him interested in an omega like me?

He came out of the bathroom in dark-blue scrubs. The top was tucked in, and the thin material gave his body virtually no protection.

I could see his abs. The thickness of his thighs. All kinds of thickness going on under the blue fabric.

"If you don't stop looking at me like that, I'll never get to the patient."

"You'd better go then because I'm having a hard time not drooling."

Chuckling, he walked over and put his hands on my shoulders. "There is a pillow and a blanket on the couch and snacks are in the bottom right drawer. Water—in the fridge." He leaned down, pressing his forehead to mine. "I'm having a very hard time leaving you right now."

"You have to. People need you. Go on. Do your job and then come back to me. I'll be fine."

He nodded and kissed my forehead and then my lips—twice. "I'll be back."

As the door shut behind him, I let out a sigh. Not the way I wanted to end this date but at least

I wasn't home alone. He would come back once he'd finished up.

I got on my phone and read some of my latest book until my eyelids drooped. The pillow and blanket smelled like Jabez, and I pressed it to my face, inhaling the vanilla and brown sugar goodness. Lying with my legs curled up on the short couch, I took a moment to let myself dream about what it would be like to be mated to Jabez. Would this be my life, waiting and hoping he was okay, not a lot of time between his two jobs?

Still, it would be worth it to have even a few moments with him.

I sighed as sleep took me. Jabez would be the best dad.

Chapter Fifteen

Jabez

I thought I'd only be an hour or so, assuming one of the on-call doctors would be able to take over once the patient was stabilized, but no such luck. The patient remained an active emergency well into the night and almost until dawn, giving me not even a few minutes to go back and send the omega home in a rideshare.

Not even time to check my phone in case he'd texted to say he'd decided to leave, but as the sun was red-lining the horizon, I opened the door to my office to find he had not left but instead had fallen asleep on my couch.

I knew it was short for me but had somehow thought his shorter stature would afford him more comfort. Seeing him curled up with his knees to his chest, I felt terrible. Despite the fact I'd been occupied with the pack alpha of a local pack who suffered from one of those rare diseases I was known for dealing with. His own healer had not known anything about it, being an older and more traditional fellow who had learned at his own mentor's knee and never studied a thing beyond what that wolf knew.

If he hadn't been brought in that night, and if they had not called in someone familiar with the issue, he'd be a dead one this morning, leaving a pack challenge in the offing.

This was why I was here. Why I hadn't hung up my stethoscope. Why I traveled so much. And...why I was such a bad choice for a mate. I should probably just enjoy his company while I could and try not to think of the day when he would realize that I wasn't worth all the waiting around.

Gods, that was going to happen, wasn't it?"

Beale didn't look very comfortable, even covered with my blanket and with his head on the pillow, but I didn't know how much sleep he might have had, so I hesitated to waken him. My office faced east and the sun as it rose would flood the room with light, helping him to wake naturally. Until then, I would just sit at my desk and take care of some paperwork. Not actual paper, of course, it was on the laptop. Same idea. Or it would have been, if I hadn't fallen asleep about two seconds after landing my butt in my chair.

Sometime later, I woke bathed in midmorning light, my exhausted self not having been disturbed by any of the earlier sunshine. But what did make me stir was the feeling of being watched.

I opened my eyes to find Beale sitting up on the sofa, the blanket folded next to him with the pillow sitting neatly atop it.

"Good morning, Jabez," he said. "I didn't hear you come in."

"I know." I rubbed my face, trying to push the last of the sleep away. "I didn't want to disturb you."

"You had a long night," he said. "I tried to stay awake, but finally I gave up, figured if I got a bit of sleep, I'd be in better shape to face the day."

"I never thought...do you work today?" If I'd made him stay up most of the night and then he had to try to do his job? That would be a very irresponsible alpha indeed.

"No, I am off until tomorrow. No need to worry, but I still owe you dinner."

"Beale, you did eat some of the snacks in my drawer, didn't you?"

He shook his head. "I forgot they were there, and then I fell asleep."

"Oh, omega, you must be starved."

"And you, Jabez? Did you find time for a meal?"

Gods, he had me again. "No, in fact I did not."

"Then we'd better head out to a restaurant somewhere for breakfast." He was on his feet and smoothing a hand through his hair. "What do you feel like?"

"How about the cafeteria here? I think you'll be surprised at how good the food is, and frankly I'm too hungry to wait very long." Even if I was willing to allow him to do so. Which I was not.

"If you like. But aren't hospitals known for bad food?" His little grimace was the cutest thing I'd ever seen.

"Human hospitals." I stood up and started for the door, grabbing his hand along the way. "If you hate it, we can eat just enough not to faint from hunger and then go anywhere else you want."

We weren't even off the elevator when the scents of bacon frying and brewing coffee met my nose.

"I didn't think a hospital would serve bacon," Beale marveled. "Let's eat."

Chapter Sixteen

Beale

Despite the rumors, the hospital cafeteria breakfast was very good. Hot, fluffy biscuits. A loaded omelet made fresh. Fresh fruit bowls. I hoped every patient there got the same breakfast, though I knew that was impossible with dietary concerns and varying ailments.

Still, I usually opted for a couple of boiled eggs with my coffee, so it was a treat for me.

"I saw what you did there," I said as we walked out of the hospital. Jabez was still in his scrubs and carried his other clothes in a duffle he kept in the office.

"Me? What do you mean?"

Fake innocence. The alpha pulled a fast one on me but there wasn't a damned thing I could do about it. He paid for dinner since we were in a hurry and then this morning, paid for breakfast under the guise of the employee discount.

"I still want to buy you a meal," I whined. I pushed out my bottom lip in a pout for good measure.

He shook his head, laughing. "Maybe you can pay me back another way."

"Maybe."

After he drove away and I was safely inside my apartment, I immediately felt the loss of his presence. I was sure he was my mate, but we hadn't said the words, only danced around them.

Next day, I worked my regular shift at the coffee shop but the whole time, my thoughts were filled with the healer alpha and how I missed him terribly. All of our dates had been cut short or accidental in nature, but what I wanted was him, all to myself, preferably naked. To strip away the titles we held and the social gap that was probably only in my mind and be with him, in the darkness. To learn all the things about him only a lover would know.

Even though I was tired and needed a night at home, I couldn't deny the pull to go see the alpha that dominated my thoughts. He texted me a few times during the day and said he would be at the club that night but didn't offer an invitation.

I knew what I wanted and it was him.

I showered the day away and got dressed for the club. I didn't have a lot of options for club attire, but I picked out my best outfit and put my coat over it. Tonight, Jabez was supposed to do another demonstration, according to his texts.

He hadn't asked me to be his demo partner and that sucked.

Just the thought of him being there, watched by others, with another omega made my skin tingle and my face flood with heat.

Goddess, I was jealous—just thinking about him with another.

Of course, as he'd drawn the wand over my skin, for me, it was more. He made eye contact. Those transfixing brown eyes bore right into my soul and even though we were being watched by dozens of people, when I was with him in the club, it was only him and me. No one else.

I parked my car a few blocks over, not using the valet. My car was a bit embarrassing, even though it took me where I needed to go and it was paid off, but compared to the other luxury cars that lined up to be parked, mine was a junker.

The attendant took my phone and instead of heading to the demo areas, I went directly to the bar.

Tonight called for a drink. My nerves were already out of control, and I was willing to spend the money for one. Drink in hand, I strolled around the club, trying to pretend I wasn't looking for one person.

I was. The only reason I kept coming back was because of Jabez. Sure, there were other alphas and other scenes I could watch or partake in, but there was only one of him.

He was the only one my wolf wanted.

I saw all kinds of scenes happening. I avoided the knife play station like the plague, not wanting to relive that night with Aaron or think of that jerk of an alpha at all.

When I got to the station where I'd found Jabez last, I froze.

There was an omega in the chair. No shirt on. Only leather pants.

And the alpha getting ready to put on a demonstration?

My alpha.

Mine.

"Oh, hell no." I gave my drink to the nearest person, who strangely took it without context, and marched into the room intending to rip that omega right from the table and replace him, with me.

"Beale, I'm so glad you came," Jabez said. "I knew you would show up. Thank you for volunteering, Jeff, but my demo partner showed up."

"Huh?" I said, watching as the omega groaned but moved away from the station. Not my smoothest moment. There were at least fifty people watching us, maybe more. They waited, like me, to see what would happen next.

Jabez reached out and brushed his knuckles over my cheek and then kissed my lips gently. "I knew you would come."

"Why didn't you just ask?" I said.

"I didn't have to. This tether between us would bring you to me—I just knew it."

Chapter Seventeen

Jabez

"Would you like to come home with me?"

"Yes." Beale never hesitated.

I asked him as soon as the scene ended. Teaching him all the things I could do with the wand, or at least many of them, had been such a bonding moment that I didn't want to wait another moment. But I also needed to clear the air about some things. I followed him home, so he could leave his car there, then drove him to my home. He followed me inside, looking around. "This is a very nice place."

"It isn't anything fancy, but it serves me." I closed the door behind us and bent to kiss him. "Do you want the tour?"

"No...is that all right?"

"You don't want to see my house?" I was confused. He'd said he liked it and I wanted him to feel comfortable here.

"I want to see you, preferably naked and on top of me."

I choked on a breath. "Omega, that's very bold of you."

"Oh...you don't like that?" He sounded so disappointed, and I didn't want that for him at all.

"No," I hastened to say before he felt any worse. "I'm very glad that you feel you can speak to me in any way you like. When we're at the club in a scene where I am the dom, even then you have all the power. You know that, right?"

"In theory, but that really hasn't been my experience."

I led him across the living room, toward the stairs. "If you're with me, that will be the case. If you use your safe word, everything stops. And more than that, before we ever scene, we will talk it out so I know what you want and what you don't, and where I can encourage you to expand your experience."

"But we didn't do all that, tonight," he said.

"No, tonight was a demo, not a full scene, and I stopped every few minutes to get guidance from you, make sure you were good with our direction, didn't I?"

He grinned. "Yes, you did. I was glad for it, but I think if we have discussed things ahead of time, it will be less stop and start, right?"

"Exactly. Now, you refused the full tour, but this is my bedroom, and I don't see how we can skip that."

"Absolutely not. This is the part I want to see." He stepped away from me and turned in a circle. "Very nice. Oh, look. There's a bed here. Mind if I try it out?"

I had not seen this side of him before, and I loved it. "Make yourself at home." I plopped down on the edge of the mattress. "I just want to tell you a little about my past. Before we do anything that you might regret if you know more about me later."

"Wait. Have you been a criminal? Killed anyone?"

"No." I hadn't done that. "But I—"

"Have you broken anyone's heart? I mean not in middle school but as a full adult?"

"No. But I..." We had had several long talks, but I had managed not to mention something important.

"Alpha, if you don't take me now, I won't be responsible for what I might do."

As an alpha dom, I had to put my omega's needs first. "I just need you to know that I was mated before and am widowed."

"Why do you need me to know? I mean, I want to know everything about you but right this second, I don't want to think of you with anyone else. But later, I want to know it all."

"I never expected there to be another for me, never even really knew that Fate would consider giving me a second."

He straddled my lap, looping his arms around my neck. "And now?"

"Now, I think I must have done something very good in another life because you are my mate." I nuzzled his cheek. "And you?"

"I only feel half alive when we're not together." He rested his head on my shoulder. "You are my mate. And I've never been mated before, but I am so honored that Fate chose you for me, and so sorry you had to go through the heartbreak of the past."

"Omega, you are the most amazingly sweet male. But way overdressed." I stood him on his feet and joined him. "Let me help you with that."

We helped one another, our clothing landing I didn't even care where, so anxious to have this male's skin against mine. Shifters weren't too worried about nudity, and at Cuffed, there were any number of people walking around nude or close to it, but with my mate?

So different. I took in his body as he revealed it, learning how he looked without clothes, memorizing the person who would be a part of my life for the rest of our lives after tonight. Then I laid him on the bed and used my hands and lips to cover the whole landscape of him before he groaned and tugged me closer. "Please, Alpha. I can't wait any more."

"You've been very patient, omega mine." I glided a hand between his cheeks. "So slick. So ready for me." Gently lifting his legs, I pressed them to his chest and found his hole with the head of my cock.

Even with all the slick, he was so tight, I had to move slowly, not wanting to hurt him until he rocked his hips, taking me halfway into him in one glide. Omegas usually were all about letting the alpha take the lead in everything, and I liked that he would be an equal in the bedroom. It was refreshing and new and made me even harder if possible.

His cock jutted out between us, and I closed a fist over it, wanting to bring him along with me. Would he want to fuck me too? I'd never done that, but the idea of that with him nearly made me come embarrassingly soon. Stroking him, I squeezed, released, and rubbed my palm over his bulbous head. My omega's heat surrounded me, as I drove into him again and again, holding back as long as possible.

Just when I didn't think I could wait, he moaned and his cum was pouring over my hand. I followed, seconds later, my knot swelling inside him.

Beale's head dropped to the side, and I bent to sink my teeth into his vulnerable throat, marking him as mine in a move I never thought I would make again.

But then I never expected to love anyone like this.

Chapter Eighteen

Beale

I woke up to the smells of eggs, vanilla, brown sugar, and cinnamon. My body was luxuriously sore in all the right places, and I felt each one as I stretched in Jabez's bed.

Jabez. My alpha. My mate. My fated one.

I reached up and touched the mark on my shoulder, the bite that meant we belonged to each other. Not for a time but forever. The bite was still tender but no longer an open wound. Instead, it felt like a scar I'd had forever.

"Good morning," the object of my thoughts spoke. I rose up to sit in the bed and saw him standing in the doorway, only wearing a pair of low-slung lounge pants. He had a spatula in his hand and a smile on his face.

"Good morning," I replied with a yawn.

"I didn't wear you out, did I?" He put the spatula on the dresser and came over to get onto the bed with me.

"Yes. But in the best way. I slept so deeply. It's been a while since I had that kind of rest."

He kissed my lips but I pulled back quickly. Morning breath was the opposite of sexy. "What's the matter, omega? Are you shy all of a sudden?"

I shook my head. "No, but I need to brush my teeth."

Jabez shook his head and laughed. "Good thing I bought a toothbrush for you a few days ago."

I got out of bed but looked back at him. "A few days ago?"

He nodded. "I've wanted you in my bed for a while now. Thought I'd prep. A man can dream, right?"

"I'm glad I wasn't the only one. Do you want to join me for a shower, or are you still cooking? French toast?"

"I finished cooking for you, mate. I was hoping to wake you up myself, but I'll settle for a nice long, hot shower."

Those words alone had me harder than steel.

"Sounds good to me."

We had a long shower that was both dirty and clean. Afterward, we put on shorts and went down to the kitchen.

"Please tell me there's coffee."

"There is coffee, but I'm afraid it's substandard compared to what you serve at the shop."

I snorted. "Do you want to know a secret?"

He came over and pulled me close. "I want to know all your secrets."

"I don't really like the coffee from my job except when it's doused in all kinds of syrups and creamers. On its own, it's overly roasted and just tastes bitter." Immediately I hung my head in shame. My name tag said barista, but I hated what I served people.

It was just a job to me—something to pay the bills.

"I'm glad I'm not the only one. I hate that stuff, too. And let's face it, the cold ones are just caffeinated milkshakes."

I threw my head back, laughing. "That's so true."

Jabez wouldn't let me get my own coffee. Instead, he insisted that I stand next to him while he learned how to make it the way I liked it. Two sugars, lots of cream, for the record. We ate stacks of French toast with bacon and blueberry syrup.

"How big is your backyard?" I asked as I finished up my second cup of coffee.

"It's a good size, why?"

"I thought we might shift. Our wolves are wanting to see each other."

"Sure. Both of my neighbors are shifters so we won't have any human prying eyes. What a great idea."

We went outside, and he was right. His yard was big enough for us to play together as our animals. In the far right corner was a hammock and a firepit. I imagined one day, we would enjoy some of those things together.

"Wanna go first?" my alpha asked.

"Sure."

I took off my pants, and although he had seen all of me the night before and then again in the shower, he licked his lips. I submitted to my wolf, letting him take over our shared form. One second, I was on two legs, and the next, I stood on four. Fur emerged from my skin. My human teeth were replaced with wolf ones, including fangs.

"Oh, omega. Look at you. How beautiful you are, little wolf." Jabez got down on one knee and ran his fingers through my fur. My wolf soaked up his praise and his touch, but he wanted to see his counterpart, his mate's wolf. We let out a yelp, a gentle nudge, and our alpha got the message right away.

"All right, impatient mate."

In seconds, Jabez shifted into his wolf. His wolf was not gray like mine but a black so dark that the sun made some of his fur seem to shimmer in dark purples. He was gorgeous and all mine.

While we couldn't run together in the confined space, we lay in the sun for a while and played. Bouncing and nipping at each other. It was almost noon by the time we shifted back. Our animals had bonded now.

"I have to go." I broke the news to him as I gathered my clothes from the night before. It felt weird to put my club clothes on if I was only going home, but I didn't plan to spend the night.

"Here." He reached into a dresser drawer and pulled out a shirt and tossed it to me. "Do you have to go? You don't even like the coffee there."

I laughed, and it warmed my heart to hear that he wanted me to stay. "I do. I have bills to pay, Jabez. I'm sure you have patients and club business as well."

Nodding, he came over, wrapping me up in a hug and kissed the top of my head. "I kind of miss you already."

"Kind of?" I teased.

"No, omega. Not kind of. I already really miss you."

Chapter Nineteen

Jabez

My wolf had wanted him closer to us from the first day, insisting he belonged in our den, but I had still been stuck in the idea that I would never want another omega in my life, that I did not deserve someone.

Treating myself like a child who is the reason a family cannot have nice things.

Overall, if I wanted to make a good life with my omega, I was going to have to forgive myself for the past, accept what my mentor and others close to me insisted, and recognize that there was nothing I could have done to save him.

And if I was going to treat my omega as my partner, I needed to show him the respect he deserved. I absolutely should have shared more about my past before we mated, but he had not wanted that, and he did know that I was widowed.

But we'd come so close now and I wanted him under my roof. I needed to be sure we could be completely open with one another. I could not survive otherwise.

So, I invited him over for dinner, hoping to clear the air of the few things that I felt needed to be said. I knew many shifters, once they met their fated, would just leap, and we kind of had done that, but as a widower, I was carrying some baggage. Even in forgiving myself, that experience had affected me and my world view.

"This is great. I never would have barbecued so early in the year, but the weather is perfect, isn't it?" Beale was sitting on a lounge chair on my patio, looking so relaxed and at home, my wolf had never been happier.

"I always enjoy grilling." I flipped the steaks and came to sit in the chair next to his. "Did you have a good day?"

"Not bad." He grinned. "I got a big tip for remembering the twenty things that went into this guy's latte."

"Was it really twenty?" My mind reeled, trying to think of what twenty things could fit in one cup of coffee. "Or just a lot."

"Twenty." He shook his head. "Although a few of them were literally a drop or two because it is not a gallon jar."

"Oh, that's so funny. You deserved that tip."

We talked a little more about our days. I'd had a patient who hadn't been expected to do well make a turn for the better, and I was glad to share that before we settled in with our plates and the sunset.

"I told you I was a widower, but I did not say that I lost him and a child at the same time. He died giving birth."

"Oh, alpha." Beale set his fork down and reached for my hand. "That must have been so hard. Just a mate is enough but a child as well?"

"He had been hiding a secret from me." I swallowed. It was so difficult to talk about even all these years later. But I had to be vulnerable and show my mate where I was coming from. In fairness. "He had a rare condition that meant pregnancy was not only dangerous but likely fatal. And he never told me. I wanted children, but we could have adopted or just enjoyed nieces and nephews. Whatever. I really took the blame for not knowing."

"How could you know? He didn't tell you."

"No, he didn't and that is why I want you to know. I want us to be honest and transparent

Lorelei M. Hart

with one another. No secrets, no lies, not even of omission."

"I promise to do my best," he said solemnly. "And I admire the strong person you are after such a heartbreaking experience.

He could have complained that I had waited to tell him, although I had tried once before. I could have tried harder and not done it when we were both so ready to tear one another's clothes off.

"I promise, too," I told him. "And if you move in here, we'll have lots of time to be transparent with one another."

"Right." He picked up his fork again and let it drop again. "Wait. What did you say?"

"I asked if you'd move in?"

Silverware clattered to the deck as he launched himself at me. I held my plate out of the way and caught him with the other arm. "Is that a yes?"

"Of course. I was just so surprised."

"Omega mine, you're my mate. Where else would you live but in my den?"

We spent the rest of the evening making plans. His lease would be up in a month, and I

112

didn't see any reason why he should stay there

just because he had to pay one month. Why wait?

I was very happy and very in love.

Chapter Twenty

Beale

Jabez had come in sometime in the middle of the night. Not a surprise. The club closed at midnight on weekdays, but there was work to be done after all the members and guests went home—and that was if there wasn't a patient in need at the hospital.

I'd heard the door of his home open and lay there listening to the sounds of my mate. He threw his keys into the bowl by the front door. Kicked his shoes off and put them in the cabinet. Jacket placed on his hook. He would stop at the sink for a glass of water and then come upstairs.

Never thought I'd take joy from lying awake in the middle of the night listening to someone do such mundane things, but I did.

He entered the bedroom softly but came over and placed a gentle kiss on my lips. "I won't be long," he whispered. His wolf would feel through the bond that I was awake. This was our routine as well.

I turned over to face Jabez's side of the bed. When he got in, we would have a bit of pillow talk about his night and my day and all the things that happened.

I hadn't gone to the club this week, not feeling like myself. I was tired all the time to the point where I had to call in sick to work the day before.

Calling into work meant something was really wrong. I considered myself a hard worker.

I'd also been sick to my stomach—a lot. Jabez didn't think I had any kind of bug or virus, but neither of us could deny that something was going on. He blamed himself. Between working and the club and our middle-of-the-night sessions once he got home, he thought I was simply worn out.

My mate showered and came to bed. The mattress dipped and, soon, he gathered me in his arms.

"How was your night?" I asked.

"Uneventful. I monitored the fire table."

"Fun," I said, already drifting back to sleep.

"Let's talk about it in the morning, omega. I can feel your exhaustion." He kissed my forehead and I snuggled in and drifted off.

Hours later, I turned over and stretched my arms over my head, but the moment I sat up, nausea swept over me.

"Oh!" I sprinted to the bathroom where I hunched over the toilet and dry heaved. Nothing but bile came from my empty stomach, but that didn't stop my body from trying.

"Beale," Jabez said, running over and coming to stand next to me.

"There's nothing," I said, flushing the toilet anyway. Not knowing what was going on with me, I began to cry.

"Come here." Jabez wrapped his arms around me, and I crumpled against him. "I had an idea about what's going on with you last night but you were so tired."

That got my attention. "What? What is it?"

"My love, I think you might be pregnant." He squeezed me tighter.

There were a couple of things to unpack in that sentence. One, he kind of said he loved me. Two, I was what?

Pregnant.

Huh.

"I need a test." Because above anyone else, I trusted my mate. He was a healer, after all. Even if he wasn't, he had great instincts.

"Would you be upset if I told you I already got one?" he asked.

"No. I would be relieved. Did you really?"

He nodded. "I left it in the car. Give me one minute."

I let the notion soak in while he was gone. Could I be pregnant? We hadn't been together long but, then again, it only took once.

Looking down at my bare stomach, I placed both hands over it. If I had a pup inside me, then I would love it with all my heart.

"I'm here."

The next few moments passed in a blur. I peed on the stick. Waited in the bedroom. Waited some more. Jabez checked his watch over and over.

Two minutes felt like a lifetime.

"It's ready," my alpha said. "Do you want to look or should I?"

"Let's do it together."

We walked back into the bathroom and I flipped over the plastic stick.

Two lines.

"I'm pregnant." The words felt like someone else was saying them.

"We're having a baby. Omega mine, are you happy?" Jabez cupped my face with his hands.

"I am. I'm so happy. Are you? I mean, the timing isn't amazing. You work so much. I..."

"Hey," he said, kissing my cheeks, bringing me out of my overthinking. "I'll do whatever it takes to be here for you and our babe. Trust me?"

I let out a long breath. "I do. I'm not asking you to quit working, Jabez."

"Of course you're not. But I can cut back some. Make some changes. You won't be in this alone. I'll always be here for you."

Fresh tears streamed down my face. "I know that. I do. I love you, mate."

"I love you, Beale. You've made me the happiest alpha by becoming my mate, but this? I never thought I'd be so happy."

Chapter Twenty-One

Jabez

Things moved very quickly once we found out Beale was pregnant. I was still scared, but also happy and excited, and determined not to let my fears govern our life together. Fate had given me another chance to live and love, and I was not going to throw it back in her face.

Especially since my omega was blossoming every day. Once he'd gotten past the first few months, the nausea faded and he became the happiest handsomest pregnant omega on the face of the planet. Or maybe I was just a little prejudiced.

Like today, when we were going to buy nursery furniture. The store didn't even open for an hour, and Beale was already in the front seat of the car, bouncing. "Hurry, alpha. I want to get there before it's all gone."

"The cribs and car seats?" Why would they all be gone?

"And the diaper bags and the dressers, bottle warmers, just everything." He tilted his head and narrowed his eyes at me. "You didn't forget, did you?"

"No. I have the list so we won't forget anything."

"That not what I mean. Today is the big sale. I told you."

He probably had. I'd been working so many hours I barely knew my own name. "I'm sorry, omega. I see why you're in a hurry to get there." I tried to make it up to him by driving through his favorite donut place, but all that accomplished was putting us at the end of a very long line of pregnant omegas and their alphas. This must be a great sale if all those pregnant people were willing to stand there like that. Beale was spending less time on his feet every day. I pulled into a parking space anyway.

"Oh no." He had his face pressed to the glass. "We are late."

"Maybe we should try another day," I suggested.

"And miss the sale?" His voice vibrated with outrage at the very idea. "Everything is 20 percent off today only." He unclicked his seat belt and climbed out of the car.

I didn't need to buy discounted furnishings, but my omega had been careful with money his whole life and since we'd decided he would quit working after he had the baby, he had doubled down in the idea of stretching a dollar. But as we took our place at the end of the line, I had my doubts about the wisdom of this particular savings plan.

"Omega mine, maybe we shouldn't do this. It's a lot of standing." And probably by the time we got into the store, all the things on our list would be gone.

"Well, you don't have to stay. I can take a rideshare home after I shop." There was that sassy omega again. "But I am not having our baby sleep in a designer crib I paid full price for." Oh yeah, not only was he into stretching that dollar, he wanted quality as well. "Besides, a bunch of these bloated omegas won't even make it until the store opens."

"Speak for yourself," the omega in front of us snapped. "I will get that car seat I've had my eyes on even if I have to stand up until my ankles become cankles and flop over my shoes." A glance down confirmed they were well on the way

to that as we spoke. Not that I was foolish enough
to say so.

After a while, the line began move forward,
the omegas ahead of us shuffling like creatures
from a zombie movie after having stood there for
who knew how many hours. Word came down
the line that the doors were open and they were
allowing people to enter. Forty-five minutes after
that, the double glass doors came into sight and
with them the chaos beyond. Omegas were
wrestling for items, alphas hugging the walls in, if
not terror, certainly discomfort. Their mates
would shove items into their arms then dive back
into the fray. Some of them were no more than
days from delivery, and if no babies were born in
there today, it would be a miracle.

"Really, Beale, I think we should give up.
Those people have already ransacked the store."

"They don't know where to find some of the
good stuff," he asserted. "I came by the other day
and took pictures then made a diagram, see?" He
held up his phone to show me. "So, here's the
plan." He laid out what he'd be doing and what I
would then tucked his phone back in his pocket
and pushed into the store.

If I never again did something like this, it would be too soon. It was not worth the money we saved. To me. To Beale, every piece in the nursery would be a triumph to remember. So it was worth the bruises and the patch of hair I was sure I was missing from when I bent down to pick up a cloth diaper from the floor that an omega thought belonged to them.

Life would never be dull with my sweet and sassy omega.

And I hoped our baby would take after him.

Chapter Twenty-Two

Beale

This was not the place where I wanted to have our baby, but after a night filled with not only my water breaking but ever intensifying contractions and pain, well, it was our only choice.

Given what Jabez had gone through with his previous mate, we'd made a plan that was full proof.

At least, that's what we'd hoped for.

I had monitors all over me. Tracking my heart rate, my blood pressure, and more all over my belly, tracking contractions and the baby's heartbeat.

A nurse came in and asked me if I wanted some ice chips to which I said yes.

Jabez was paler than I'd ever seen him and gripping my hand as though he were the one in labor instead of me.

"Is something wrong with the baby?" I asked him.

"They are monitoring his heartbeat. That's all."

Didn't seem normal to me, but he was the healer.

The nurse returned with the ice chips and had another healer. Neither of them was smiling.

That couldn't be good.

"Beale, we've got some concerns. As your labor progresses, your baby's heartbeat is slowing. I don't think they are handling all of this well."

Jabez swallowed and gripped the edge of the bed.

"I understand. What's the plan?" I asked, hoping my voice somehow drowned out the pounding of my heart.

"We think the best course of action is a C-section. Not my first choice for birth, but we are going to do what's best for you and your baby. Jabez, I'm sure you agree."

"Yes," he choked out. My poor alpha. I was sure he was reliving part of his trauma right then and there. "As long as they are both healthy, we'll do whatever. Right?" He looked down at me, tears welling in his eyes.

"Yes. I think that's best. Let's make sure everyone is taken care of. We're going to be okay, mate. I promise you. I won't leave you."

"Please don't," my alpha said, only a faint shake in his voice.

"I'm gonna try my best."

On our way to the operating room, my blood pressure rose. Once I was on the table, our baby's heartbeat became more erratic with every passing moment. Jabez held my hands as I was given an epidural, and I soon had zero feeling from the chest down which was scary but also a relief. No more pain sounded like the best thing in the world.

The second-best thing would be the sounds of our pup's first cry.

"Jabez, did you want to watch or stay up there with your mate?" the surgeon asked. The other healer was in the room as well, but he would take care of our baby once they were born while the surgeon would tend to the C-section.

"I will stay here." He hovered over my face, whispering all things encouraging and telling me how much he loved me, but a tsunami of worry rose between us. Who could blame him? Fate and life had dealt him a ton of trauma in the past.

He'd told me one night that he didn't think he would be able to live through another mate dying.

Nor another baby.

He was surprised he had made it through the first round.

I listened to the surgeon's explanation. There was a ton of tugging and pressure and awkward jerks and despite Jabez being next to me, his eyes were on my belly.

Our whole family was there in that room, and our lives hung in the balance. Even the one who had no physical part in the birth.

"And there we are. We have a baby."

I listened while Jabez sucked in a breath. We listened and listened for what seemed like a million years until I heard it.

The first cries of our baby.

Jabez had never looked more torn. His body swayed a bit toward our baby, but then he looked down at me. Tears rolled down his beautiful face in relief and joy, but I knew he wouldn't be fully happy until the healer assessed our baby.

"Is it a boy or a girl?" I asked.

"A son." Jabez brushed some sweat from my forehead. "We have a son, omega."

I sighed. A son. "Go on. Go make sure he's okay. I'm fine here. I promise I'm fine."

Again, he looked torn.

"Jabez, go. Go count his toes and fingers and make sure he's breathing. I need to know too."

"I'll be back."

My mate rushed over to where I could see our son in a clear plastic crib. He was being weighed and measured and was none too happy about the experience either.

Listening to his cries while the surgeon closed me up, I thanked the gods old and new for their blessing.

The healer swaddled our babe, and Jabez brought him over.

"Is he okay?" I asked.

"He is perfect. And you are as well. Everything went fine."

I lifted another prayer of thanks. "Let me see him, please."

Not easy since I was still lying down, being stitched or stapled up. Which one, I wasn't sure.

Jabez brought our son down for me to look at. He had my nose but my mate's beautiful brown eyes. The second my mate pressed our babe's face next to mine, all crying stopped.

"He knows his daddy," Jabez whispered.

"I love you," I said to both my son and my mate.

"And we love you."

Chapter Twenty-Three

Jabez

I hadn't taken a vacation in years. Not since I lost my first mate, almost as if by working extra hard, I could make up for the horrible thing that happened. Or maybe it was partly that I didn't handle quiet times well. But I hadn't even had a nightmare in months. Life with Beale and our beautiful son was so special it seemed ungrateful to allow the wallowing of my past. And as the time I'd taken off for paternity leave was winding to a close, I wanted to do something to mark that finish in a big way.

I had heard from Rally recently as well. He and Ouro and the baby were off the streets and getting what they needed. That omega had come so close to losing his life, but he had not. He had survived and to all accounts begun to thrive. That birthing had been an echo of the trauma that nearly broke me—but it turned out fine. And that contributed to my peace of mind.

The beach house was right on the sand, and we had it for two weeks. Of course, the baby would have no memories of this, but it was such an incredible time for us to all bond as a family. I'd already made changes in my work life, with my new apprentice starting as soon as I got back. It would take time, but eventually he would be a big help. And with Beale being a full-time stay-at-home daddy, we could find time together without worrying about his work schedule. My fellow owners all incorporated the club into their lives, and a few of them also had families, so we were flexible with one another.

Sitting on the porch with Kirby on my lap, I watched Beale run down to the water and dive in. Who knew he was such a water guy? Since we'd been here, he had been swimming, surfing, body boarding, kite surfing...and he swore when the baby was old enough, he'd teach him to sail. I could see we'd be coming here for vacations every year.

"Your daddy is going to have you swimming before you're a year old, little one." I held him up so he could see Beale splashing around. "He's the fun one in this family."

And the perfect antidote to my constant soul-searching. Well, he and Kirby were. Loving them, caring for them, occupied my mind in a beautiful way.

I settled back to watch him swim. No matter how good someone was in the water, my grandmother always said never swim alone. With the baby, I couldn't go in with Beale, but our son and I could for sure be lifeguards, watching to be sure he was all right. I was not a mental case anymore over the past, but I would always be a vigilant alpha.

After a while, Beale came back up the beach and dried off before taking the baby to feed him. We'd gotten so lucky finding this beach where there were not a ton of people constantly passing us. It wasn't deserted, but there was still an intimacy that a big tourist area would not have. In fact, the Realtor told us that every place within a half mile was rented to shifters, meaning, we could get out there at night and be wolves, if it suited us. They even had recommended local babysitters, which we might take them up on. Next time.

For now, we wanted one of us at least with Kirby all the time. His first sitters would be people we knew well, and the very best thing I could imagine doing was sitting here on a

beautiful afternoon with my family and enjoying

the sea breeze.

Epilogue

Theo

"Long night?" the sitter asked when I came in. He was a young man familiar with the club. The other owners let me come in as late as possible so the sitter only had to watch my son while he slept, but that meant I didn't return home until almost three in the morning.

Bringing Abel to school after that was murder, but I would do anything for my son. Being more involved meant I had a say in what happened at the club. With so many alphas having families now, they needed more owners who could work late. Made sense.

"You have no idea."

"Thank you for the payment. You are the only one who pays a week in advance."

I scoffed and grabbed some cashews from the pantry. "You show up every night I need you, and I don't have to worry about my son while I'm at work. It's worth it to pay you in advance. I don't want you finding another job."

He grunted. "I get to study while Abel sleeps and you get to work. Finding a job that's this flexible is hard when you're in school."

My babysitter was a college kid, which was why I always gave him a little bonus.

"I know. I remember."

The sitter packed up his books and headed out, locking the door on his way. I could count on him, and that was important.

Not only for my son but in life.

Counting on someone, I'd learned, didn't come easy for me after my husband left us. All my trust in omegas, humanity, and life itself died the moment he told me he was leaving us.

How he could walk away from our son was still a mystery to me.

I went to bed and went through the motions the next day, but though I still had resentment in my heart, I was lonely. The other owners at the club had found love and trust with their omegas.

Perhaps there was a part of me that could trust again, but mostly, I wanted another father for Abel.

He didn't understand where his papa went. It took him three months not to cry every night for him.

It broke my heart and hardened it against loving ever again.

An Excerpt from Such a Delicious Omega

On the other side of death is light and life. When
I almost died after being in the wrong place at the
wrong time, I decided it was time to start living
and stop simply surviving and live my best life.
So, I sat down with my friends and made a list of
all the things I'd always wanted to do or be.

My friends appeared shocked by the items I
penned. The friend they'd known for so many

years would think twice before wearing a bright-colored shirt. And yet, I listed skydiving, bungie jumping, flying all the way to Japan to eat blowfish. And I did those things, checking them off as I went. On the tamer side, I rode a horse and took tango lessons. Until only one thing remained on my list.

Visit a dungeon. A kink club lay in the city only a few miles away. It was members only, with exceptions made for guests or, of course, those interested in joining. Was I interested in joining? I'd never know until I tried. If only I had an alpha to go with.

Such a Delicious Omega is the fourth book in His Alpha Desires, the highly anticipated M/M Mpreg shifter series by USA Today Bestselling Author Lorelei M. Hart and featuring the members and staff of the hottest new club in town. Such a Delicious Omega features a new alpha club owner intrigued by the newbie omega guest at Cuffed, sweet heat, sizzling heat, new beginnings, finding oneself, true love, fated mates, an adorable baby (or two) and a

guaranteed HEA.

Chapter One

Echo

"I'm gonna throw up and piss my pants." I turned to see my friend Zack turn a putrid shade of green as he watched the instructors and pilot put all the gear into the plane and do the last-minute safety checks.

Fear hadn't overlooked me. Its hooks were in my chest making me struggle for every breath, but I'd learned to sink into the feeling instead of running from it.

At least, when it came to things on my list.

"You gotta pick one," I said over the sounds around us. The smaller airport only served private flights and skydiving expeditions, but it sure was noisy. "Throw up or pee. You can't have both."

Zack laughed, pushing his dark-brown hair out of his face to no avail. It always managed to find its way back into his eyes. He'd drawn the short stick in coming with me but, at the same time, my group of friends insisted I go with someone. They had worried themselves sick when I was in Japan on my own. "Let's talk about something else. You need to add to your list. You've only got two things left."

"This and... I forgot the other one."

"No, you didn't, Echo. Hell, I didn't forget, and it's not my list."

I nodded as the hooks of fear dug in deeper. Sure, jumping out of an airplane with nothing but a parachute was terrifying, but the last thing on my list made my stomach turn.

Visit a dungeon. A sex club.

Goddess, the only experience I had with dungeons was from my Google searches and romance novels. I could guess some things I wouldn't like. Electric play. Those violet wands with all the crazy tips I saw when I looked them up scared me. Fire play. Even scarier.

"The dungeon," I muttered, shuddering at the name alone.

"Have you even looked one up yet? Is there a good one in the city?"

"I don't know," I answered. "I'll do all that once I get this crossed off."

Zack stared off into space. His coloring wasn't so green anymore. Maybe all he needed was a change of subject. "You don't have to do

146

any of this, you know. No one would hold it against you."

I snorted. "Are you sure? You and James and Amber are the ones who helped me make it. I...I feel like I need to finish it."

My friend turned to me, hands on his hips. "Well, here we go. Look."

The instructor waved us over. We got onto the plane, and the rest was a blur. The roar of the plane. The yelling from the team as they went over the instructions and safety measures one more time. My stomach did a somersault as they opened the door, giving us a view of the vast expanse we were about to fling ourselves into. The view was spectacular. Looking over the weaving lines of land and water, as though viewing a huge puzzle.

Why was I doing this?

Why did I keep looking death in the face while trying to run from its snares?

We leapt from the plane and thankfully both landed safely on the ground. The rush I'd gotten from jumping and soaring through the sky had given me a temporary reprieve from the clamp on my chest, but as soon as we got back into our street clothes and headed to lunch, the vise grip had strengthened once again.

Making the list—the bucket list—had, at first, been a way of making sure the things I wanted to do were done before I died.

Because after almost dying at the hands of the ocean, I realized how short and fragile life was. We took it for granted, of course—me included. I'd been skirting through life before the boating accident.

Why I thought sailing was a good idea in the first place, I didn't know.

Kendall, my friend who owned the boat, still had a look in his eyes when we talked about that night. He carried some guilt about what happened to me even though I'd told him over and over that it was an accident. I'd fallen off the boat and hit my head on a buoy in the process, rendering me unconscious for just enough time to almost drown. The night had made the water almost black, so no one could see me to save me.

I'd saved myself—barely. My parents said Fate dragged me from the depths. My friends thought the Goddess had saved me for a purpose.

Me? I assumed I was just lucky. No matter the reason—I wasn't wasting one more moment of my life.

But no more sailboats. Not in a million years.

"Where'd you go?" Zack asked as we made our way to lunch. Part of the deal with him skydiving with me was a lunch of his choice afterward.

"Just thinking."

Over lunch, we kept the subject light until Amber asked how the trip went. All my friends were fixated on the last thing on the list while I was scrambling for things in my head to fill the void—adding to the list. More running toward goals meant sprinting away from what happened to me and the aftermath.

"So...let's talk about the dungeon," Zack said, swirling the last of his wine in his glass.

"I've got to start researching. The last thing I want to do is to go to a sleazy place. I want to find an upscale club. One that's safe."

"Oh!" Cam, another one of my friends exclaimed. "I know of a place. My last date brought me there. It's not something I'm interested in, but it is definitely a good one. It is called Cuffed. Google it. It's only a short rideshare away."

I sighed. "Okay. Let's do this."

Chapter Two

Samuel

I never thought I'd be an owner.

I'd worked hard every day of my adult life and most of my teens, but the buy-in for Cuffed was still miles beyond my budget. As I signed and initialed a hundred times it seemed then handed the iPad to Alex on my left. He and the other owners had been bosses but also friends in the few years since Cuffed opened. It was an honor just to work there, and I'd have gladly stayed in my position as long as they were willing to have me. Not bad for a guy like me who grew up on the wrong side of the tracks and got my GED so I could leave school early and help my mom support my younger brother and sister during my dad's long, final illness.

It was a lot for a kid, but I never resented it. Pops had been sick as long as I knew him, but he never failed to have a good word or a smile for us. Even when he could barely lift his head from the pillow, he wanted to hear about my brother's debate or my little sister's basketball game.

He passed before they finished high school, but it was my honor to see to it they went to college and got started in life. Mom remated, the kids were launched, and I was finally able to explore the lifestyle that had called to me all along.

From the first night Cuffed was open, I knew I'd found my people. The only question was how I'd managed to get along for so many years without it. Well, I knew how. Family came first; my father counted on me. My eyes still welled up when I remembered the look in his eyes on that last day, when he no longer had the power of speech, but I knew what he was asking.

"I've got this, Dad. It's no trouble to take care of the people we love."

"Samuel?"

"What?" Hell. I'd nearly missed one of the most important moments of my life woolgathering. "Sorry. I was just thinking of my dad and how he'd be so proud of me for becoming an owner of such a successful business."

"Even this one?" Bronson chuckled. "He must be a very enlightened male."

"He was, although we never talked about lifestyle matters. But he never failed to support any of us."

"Was?" Bronson patted my hand. "I'm sorry. I didn't realize your father was no longer with us."

I shrugged. "I guess I never mentioned it." It was a difficult subject for me.

"Well, wherever he is, he's proud of the way you helped the business succeed from day one, and we couldn't be happier to have you as a partner."

The others passed the iPad from one to the next, electronically signing the contract that made me an equal owner with the rest. No, I couldn't afford it on my own, but the grandfather, the pack alpha my father had never so much as spoken of, had left me an inheritance. One large enough to buy into the business and live comfortably for the rest of my life. The alpha position was mine, as well, if I chose to fight for it, but why would I do that? I didn't know anyone there, had only visited once for the reading of the will, and nothing about the others who showed up for the occasion made me want to be in charge of them.

When the document was signed by all, they handed the device back to me to hit send. Although at least one of the owners was a member of the Bar, we—wasn't that a great word, we?—used an uninvolved attorney for our legal matters in most cases. He would file all the relevant paperwork adding me into the corporation and whatever else was needed.

"Okay." I sat back, feeling a little stunned by how fast it had all happened. "I guess I'd better get to work."

"You sure you want to do this?" Alex asked. "If you'd rather not, we can hire a bar manager."

"Like what?" I considered. "You all use your skills to handle a share of the load around here, and what else would I do? Unless you don't think I've done a good job with the bar?" I thought I had, but probably most people felt as if they handled their duties well. The owners—the other owners—might have held back from commenting while I was a lowly employee, but I hoped they would feel free to comment now.

"Anything you think you might enjoy." Talon offered me a stern look. "That's the point of being an owner. Of course, you did an excellent job as bar manager, but it's up to you."

Studying the conference table in front of me, I said, "I like the position. So, if it's all the same to you, I'll stay in it."

A whoosh of air had me jerking my head up to take them all in. "What was that?"

"Relief," Alex replied. "You'd be tough to replace, but we didn't want you to feel compelled to stay as bar manager. Not only are you great with the customers and planning special events, but the employees are devoted to you."

"They just like watching me spank the naughty subs."

"And that, too."

About the Authors

Lorelei M. Hart is the cowriting team of USA Today Bestselling Authors Kate Richards and Ever Coming. Friends for years, the pair decided to come together and write one of their favorite guilty pleasures: Mpreg. There is something that just does it for them about smexy men who love each other enough to start a family together in a world where they can do it the old-fashioned way.

Sign up for our Newsletter here.

Check out the Shifters of Distance

Lorelei's Amazon Page

Made in the USA
Middletown, DE
22 March 2025

73108522R00097